THE VILLAGE OF STRONG BRANCHES

Kaye Boesme

Aigletos Press

2023

eBook ISBN 9781735740638

Print ISBN 9781735740645

This book was published by the author under Aigletos Press.

Contact information is available at kayeboesme.com

❧

For the Goddess who is

Magna Mater,

Rhea,

and Kybele,

❧

and for all of us here

navigating hard choices

and seeking to become better.

❧

CHAPTER ONE

THE YEAR AFTER her best friend died on assignment, Keð went home to Asraqan, Mamltaqal, for the festival of the dead.

It was just before midnight in Dukkă, and the platform was quiet as she waited for the train to come in, snow gently falling. Almost everyone was tethered to one of the network stations, downloading data they needed for the long journey south, but Keð had already queued up her movies and books while finalizing paperwork. One of them had to be the officer she was sharing with — a man in his forties, Vait, from Kotakl. He was stationed in the hinterlands about three hundred kilometers from Dukkă and reported to the same office, but they had never met.

Nobody on the platform looked to be from Kotakl. The train was already at horizon, its lights catching on the swirling snow.

As the train slowed to pull into the platform, a few more travelers appeared from below. People scrambled to put away their data cables. Keð connected hers only then. She had to sever her connection to the Sentinel robots in Dukkă — fifteen seconds of work for a wireless pulse. Her heartbeat was her own problem now. She was on vacation.

There was still no sign of the other officer when she boarded. Their sleeper car was spacious, at least — a bunk bed on one side, a table to sit on the other, with plenty of storage space for her carry-on. She threw it onto the rack and sat down in the seat with her tablet.

The doors rang the closing alarm twice. Just after the second one, a man opened the door to Keð's cabin — salt-and-pepper hair disheveled, medium-brown skin slightly ruddy, chest heaving — and he smiled. "You're Keð Teðqawo Qamalin?"

"Vait Aro Desin?"

He nodded twice and shut the door behind him, then immediately went to lay on the bed, still wearing a coat covered in melting snow and shoes smeared with the dirty sludge of Dukkǎ's winter streets. Keð flinched, but said nothing. Vait outranked her in the international military force, the *BC*. Even if they were both on leave, she could be reported to her supervisor for talking back.

Vait leaned up on his elbows and struggled out of his coat. He threw it onto the floor between them. The train started to move, its speed increasing quickly. It would take twenty-three hours to reach Asraqan.

"I'm going to sleep in about half an hour," Keð said.

"Too wired," Vait said. His Mamltab was lightly-accented, each *ð* a *v*, his *u* lax. "I'll make sure to have in headphones."

He smiled again. The twenty-three hours might not be so bad, Keð decided, even if Vait was a slob.

The night passed quietly. By the time she awoke seven hours later, they had gone from the 62nd parallel — Dukkǎ's latitude — to the hilly farmlands of Mamltaqal's 40th parallel, still snowy. The small announcement screen showed that they were forty-five minutes from the next stop, Bonaqan.

It left enough time for Keð to shower and get dressed. Vait slept through all of her noise, the blankets tangled, chest bare. His coat still lay in the middle of the floor.

She ordered food through the window once they reached the platform — popped nuts with to-go cups of stew, hot qumsa, and porridge — and set it out neatly on the table. She kept the window open, listening to the vendors. Vait groggily sat up. Keð was too busy looking outside to interact. She hadn't come home in two years, not since the last trip with Wiren. Nothing had changed. No new slang had crept into Mamltab. The facades of restaurants and stores just beyond the train station still needed paint to touch up the fading lettering and warping wood.

The train lurched forward again minutes later, and she leaned back in her chair to close the window. Vait wrapped one of the sheets around himself and came to sit down across from her. He opened the stew she'd given him, stuck out his tongue in disgust, and pushed it into the center of the table. "I'll stick with porridge. You should've asked me."

Keð opened her own. It was fragrant, with spices brought up from Mamltaqal's south — the ghost of home. "You were asleep."

Vait stuck his spoon into the porridge. He salted it and poured some of the qumsa — more than half — into his cup. Keð took the remainder.

The two ate in silence. Vait huddled around his food like a wild thing. It was dismissive, and she wasn't about to take that, so she opened her tablet and started looking over the correspondence her sister Tantas had sent her before leaving.

She scrolled past information about the restaurants she wanted to visit and the events happening in Asraqan to the details of their getaway retreat. Their parents, not them, had booked it. Qoziðamn was at 38th parallel like Bonaqan. This early in spring — thirteen days from now — it would be chilly, with frosts at night. Keð wished she could have stayed in Asraqan. The mini-trip meant fleeing the spring that bloomed over the low-latitude hills and mountains.

"Wow, pretty," Vait said, mouth full of food.

"She's my sister."

Vait nodded twice. "People say you're one of the officers who still tries to make nice with the family back home — you were a townie at the Academy, right?"

"You're not in touch with your family?"

"I send my sister's kids gifts sometimes," Vait said. "None of us ended up that close. Boarders are on campus the entire year, you know. Brief visitations. Is your sister married?"

Keð strained to keep smiling. The marriage was the whole reason she had to go on the retreat — she'd missed the wedding. Tantas' spouse was named Zoðr, an atan-gender water treatment operator, and she hadn't looked up anything about lim on purpose — partly out of guilt. "Yes," she said. "Chain-lineage, so just the two of them together, continuing on our family name."

"Kids?"

"They had an ova fusion just now."

"Is she or the atan carrying it? It'd be in the all-access profile, you know."

"How do you know her spouse is an atan?"

"Everyone in the BC checks files. Don't worry about it. I didn't look up your deepest secrets."

"I don't check those when it's not work-related. It's creepy, isn't it?" She paused — Vait was opening his mouth to speak, she really shouldn't have called him *creepy*, and she had to stop the conversation. "What are you doing while you're on leave?"

"Windsurfing at a resort with a classmate on the islands, 15th counter-parallel. It'll be beautiful."

Keð had never been to the southern hemisphere. It was expensive — requiring boat, not a train. It sounded better than Qoziðamn. "Sounds nice. I'm gonna catch up on some shows, would you mind if I put in my headphones?"

"Fine, if you don't want to talk."

She finished breakfast quickly and went back up to her top bunk. Vait paced for a while, and then he did the kinds of stretches and bodyweight exercises that the BC preferred they do every day even when not on duty — Keð had forgotten them, but there was still enough time in the day to do them later.

They avoided each other until early afternoon eleven stops later, when the train's staffing change happened at 28th Parallel. It was a thirty-minute service rest, long enough for the train to connect to tether. Keð and Vait both went to the table and plugged in their devices. He still wasn't dressed.

She had three messages from her sister, two from her parents. One from Bhamsǎ, her Dispatcher, who was doing recruiting circuits at the Academies to identify top-choice officers for the Dukkǎ BC Force. Some low-priority BC chatter.

"You say your sister's chain-lineage?"

"Yeah."

"But you're just using the permissions-based profile. She must not say anything about her marriage status when you're viewing it as *you*, right? Have you ever thought that's weird?"

Keð paused. "We had a fight over a girl when we were teenagers. It—"

Vait laughed, and she fell silent.

He handed her his tablet. Her hands felt unclean just holding it — it was so greasy — and the Stream profile of her sister was in unlocked view. It said *sinåmn* in the marital status — a grouping of 4-6 adults in union with one another, which meant the foundation of a new family line, not the 2-3 adults in a common chain-lineage marriage. All chain-lineage families came from a sinåmn root, though, and honored that root in the ancestral ceremonies. Keð's family had been chain-lineage for the past eleven generations.

"A baby in a sinåmn marriage is a big deal," Vait said. "Aren't the co-generation people left in the chain lineage supposed to participate in the severance ritual after its birth? Naming ceremony, right?"

Keð didn't want to talk about this on vacation. Vait was nearly a stranger. "Could we drop—"

"It won't be untethered from Qamalin until—hey!"

Keð threw the tablet down on the table. Her hands were shaking from anger, and she might throw up. "I'm sorry," she said, and she jumped to her feet.

He didn't stop her. The bathroom lay down the hall. He'd done this deliberately to hurt her, to open wounds she didn't want to discuss — did he even know about Wiren, that was the question — and the disaster of what was happening with her sister was now worse than she thought. How would she ever even fix this?

She had no memory of reaching the bathroom or of splashing water in her face. She was staring just past her reflection, water dripping from her nose and chin into the basin, hands wet, frigid. Just past her reflection was Wiren. The apparition mouthed something. She didn't know—

"Are you okay?"

Thrown back into herself, it wasn't her friend. This was another woman, with a different voice and a different face — a birthmark on her cheek — and skin about as black as Keð's. In fact, she didn't look like Wiren at all.

"Fine," she said. "Sorry, I didn't lock the door."

Keð dried her hands and stumbled back into the corridor. She leaned against the wall and breathed to calm herself down.

The festival of the dead was coming. It was natural to get spooked like that.

When she got back to the room, the tablets were gone, replaced by a spread of food — the early spring cuisine of the southern regions of Mamltaqal. Fried rectangles of flatbread lay in the center of the table, with small to-go cups of bitter green sauces and shredded fuchsia pickles beside them. A small box held fish steamed in sea-plant leaves.

Vait hadn't touched any of it — he must have been waiting for her. Stopped, it would have been easy for him to file a complaint with Bhamsă — maybe that had been his intention all along — but he just gestured at her to sit down across from him. He even served her.

6

Most of these foods were Keð's favorite. Her stomach didn't want her to eat, but her eyes did. She looked up at Vait. "I'm sorry."

"If she'd told you, you could have deferred your leave. They'll probably not let you come down for it," Vait said. "If you want some tips from my many years of service, try this one — your family sacrificed you for the service when you were committed to attend the Academy. They're not *yours* anymore, and you're not *theirs*. Your parents literally signed you away, and you owe them nothing."

Keð picked up a fork and poked at the fish.

"Do you even know what you want? You're what, late twenties? Coasting, right? Hoping it will all work out."

"It's not really that simple," Keð said.

"*Why* not?"

Keð didn't know what to say to him. She studied her plate. Her womb-mother had made things like this from scratch once upon a time, when Keð was a toddler. The fish of Keð's infancy had always been sweet, always freshwater from the lake just outside of town. "You could pull up the data if you wanted."

"Data isn't a story."

"I owe them," she said. "It's complicated."

Vait raised his eyebrows and puffed air through his lips. He served his own plate and said, "If *they* came from across the stars, you might have to choose between saving your sister and defending the world. That's what we're here for."

"I'm more afraid of what we have around us than of aliens," Keð said.

"Insurgents. You're afraid of insurgents."

"No. Earthquakes. Tsunamis. Landslides. Avalanches. The Goddess of the Mountains. You can at least try to calm *people* down. Goddesses and boulders don't listen."

Vait snickered. "Right. I'm being candid here, not critical, but who the fuck knows how they brought *you* into the service."

She only had a few more hours trapped on the train with him. "Could we talk about something else?" She held back asking him to put on clothes.

"No, I want to talk about this." Vait wiped his hand across his mouth and reached for more of the fried flatbread. He touched several pieces before making a selection. "You could petition if you really wanted to. Your Dispatcher may give you an extra week or so for exemplary service. Quick turnaround, though. You wouldn't have enough time once you got back to file."

Keð tried to picture asking Bhamsă for more time — the frown creasing into the lines of ler face, the steady gaze that said *no* even before she'd said anything. It would look like favoritism. Keð and Bhamsă were not supposed to be sleeping together, but they were. It would quickly come out if something like that happened.

"You look like I just asked you to eat rotten *ðụtl*."

"I'll think of something," she said.

Keð detrained in downtown Asraqan after another hour of strained conversation and several more of flat-out avoidance without a screen to help her. It was long after sunset, and she scrambled to finish packing her overnight bag in time to detrain. Vait handed her tablet back to her as she was leaving and promised that he'd see her again. He called her *likable*.

It was humid outside and fifteen degrees centigrade. She tethered into the connection pole on the platform, trying to hold back her anger. Bhamsă would say that keeping him out of her way was favoritism, too — and if she said anything, they might even be scheduled for the same train *every* leave.

Updates rushed onto the tablet's screen. Keð registered her presence in Asraqan with BC. She checked her messages. The five urgent ones all dealt with logistical report information. Someone else on the team would have to deal with them.

A new message had come in from Bhamsă — a constellation of characters designed to look like a smiling face. It was geolocated to Asraqan. Keð had been so preoccupied setting up things with her sister that she hadn't fully processed that Bhamsă had come *here* to interview candidates from the local BC training academy, not Zaqan or Dăyí. It was the right time of year, just after the final exams.

Let's meet up if you're not busy, Bhamsă wrote. Le used informal Mamltab. BC Dispatchers discouraged high levels of formality in Mamltab among the BC graduates from Asraqan and Zaqan's schools. Saying *sanquar-esać?* (your opinion, yes?) instead of *lăt*, *lătet*, or *lătar* (no) could get someone killed on a high-stakes mission. The lack of routine formality made it hard to tell if this was a social thing or an order.

Keð messaged back, *I'll see what Tantas says — she has plans for the festival.* A lump caught in the back of her throat when she pressed send. The void of the message box blinked up at her. In the station, her family would be waiting, unmoored from the Stream with no idea where she was. Keð wrote out ten messages of varying lengths to Bhamsă before settling on, *I miss you*, in Sò Găms, Bhamsă's native language.

The throngs of people letting out from the train had all but dissipated into the luggage queue downstairs by the time she untethered. Keð looked over the rail. The crowd oscillated in the station's atrium, its edges chaotic from those breaking free towards their platforms or pouring in. The line at the luggage station stretched around one of the pillars.

Tantas and their parents stood in the waiting area with two atan. Her ŏgam-gender parent craned ler neck up looking for Keð. One of the atan held an immaculately-lettered sign and a crown-wreath of woven, fuchsia leaves. When her father saw her, they waved at each other. She felt nauseous again, but smiled and waved back.

Her heavy boots thunked on the stairs as she went down to meet them. The insulation would make her feet a sticky, sweaty mess soon. The queue for luggage looked so long.

Her oğam-parent and father both gave her warm hugs. The two atan stayed silent until Keð approached Tantas and stretched a cursory arm around the younger sibling's shoulder.

Tantas said, "Hey." The smile was genuine.

Keð pulled Tantas into a hug and held her close. "I missed you so much." She had to fight not to say anything else, especially not in front of their parents. There was no avoiding that Tantas was in a sinåmn house now that Keð would be staying with them.

Tantas nodded and pulled away, eyes shining with tears. She jerked her head towards the atan farthest away from her. "That's Zoðr. The other one is Qentas."

Zoðr and Keð nodded at each other. The former had loose, dark hair, light brown skin, and geometric tattoos that made stylized triangular patterns all along ler chin and cheeks. It marked lim as a northerner. Atan in Asraqan typically wore their hair in braids like Qentas and stuck to tattoos immediately below their mouths. Zoðr crowned Keð with the wreath awkwardly, nearly poking her in the eyes with the branches.

"Family friend?" Keð asked. It didn't sound rehearsed, at least — she was grasping at broken seeds.

"Um," Tantas said. "So, I wanted to tell you face-to-face, except things got out of hands when you and I weren't talking to each other, but we're, um, we're all in a family together. It's sinåmn."

Keð looked at her oğam-parent. Le gave her a *look*, as if Keð might have an outburst. She'd already had one on the train. Right now she just wanted to scream, not yell. The station's ceiling far overhead felt too close, pressing down. "I need to see how the luggage line is going," she said.

"You're not even going to say—"

"Congratulations," Keð said. "You didn't even tell me. Look, I'm tired, and I just want—"

"I meant you're not even going to apologize," Tantas said.

Keð pursed her lips together. Their father said, "You've hit her with a lot. It's late. Can't you two just call a ceasefire and be done with it?"

"We really do want you here," Tantas said.

"I want to be here," Keð said. "You could have told me—"

"Just drop it," their father said. "Can you get your luggage on your own, Keð?"

"This one can help." Zoðr smiled anxiously, the fingers of ler left hand dancing. Ler northern accent treaded clumsily through cosmopolitan Mamltab consonants, complete with a habit of converting *b* and *q* into click consonants that Keð could only mimic on their own, never in words. Le continued, "This one hopes it's okay to use the familiar."

Keð wanted the answer to be *soon*, not *yes*. Even if this was her sister's spouse, they hardly knew each other. Keð looked at her parents. Her oğam-parent made a pointed glance that Zoðr couldn't see. She'd have to do it. "Go ahead."

Zoðr relaxed and grinned widely. Le put ler hands in the deeper pockets of ler chlorophyll green *mrbas*, a skirt worn by men and atan who either didn't work or preferred labor that kept their hands soft. The mrbas reached Zoðr's knees and was held at the waist by a sun-yellow sash. Le wore five bleached wood necklaces that tapped against ler flat chest as le moved. Zoðr's job was all she knew about lim.

Keð followed the signs to the luggage pickup. Neither said anything until they rounded the corner to the freight elevator and queued up. Another out-of-town train would come within the next ten minutes, swelling the line like a river during coastal storms.

"How'd you meet my sister?" Keð asked.

"A few kids in my neighborhood were stealing ID cards to engage with mature content two, three years ago," Zoðr said. "Mine was taken. I made an accident in the refreshment area that she had to troubleshoot."

Keð's brow furrowed. She tried to imagine a police station. Only those in Dukkă came to mind, alphatonal characters frosted onto bulletproof glass walls, waiting rooms lined with robotic therapy booths and vending machines for hot soups and drinks. She'd never seen the guts of a police station in Mamltaqal even though her sister worked in one. "What do you mean?"

"So, they auto-dispense qųmsa, and I somehow broke the machine, so it was spraying hot qųmsa everywhere. It was really embarrassing." Zoðr laughed.

They moved forward in line. Ahead, the station's utility robots zipped this way and that, locating passengers' luggage in the mounds that had been delivered down through the elevators. A lone security attendant oversaw everything, baton at her waist. Civic police and security guild members never carried guns like Keð, and only Keð could activate Sentinel military robots. Those would be in the station somewhere, far removed from where passersby could gawk at them, dormant. It was best to keep from thinking about things that could kill more than sixty people per minute.

She raced to think of something conversational. "Tell me about your family, Zoðr. What kind of parents do you have? Siblings?"

"One brother. Two fathers. We moved here with sinåmn housemates when I was thirteen."

"Were your dads leaving a chain-lineage house?"

"No." Zoðr scratched the back of ler head and shifted uncomfortably. "Your parents were the first lineage family I knew well. And I guess that won't continue, given that we decided to housemate."

Keð shrugged. "Honestly? We're in eleventh gen, and that's borderline unhealthy." A twinge of guilt gripped her belly, and she looked away.

It wasn't borderline unhealthy — it was tradition. She and Tantas had promised each other when they were kids that they wouldn't break the chain. She had to say what she didn't believe anyway. BC's policy on long family lines was that they destabilized local, regional, and state-level governments. Admittedly, most of the people Keð had arrested came from family lines at least fifteen generations old who thought they were above Blackout law.

Zoðr's grating chuckle startled Keð enough for her to make eye contact again. Zoðr said wryly, "Bullshit. Taboos on too many family generations are just a radical reading of *Impermanence* that people seem to like down here."

"I see." Keð waved her ID towards one of the robots. It scanned Keð's card and went off in search of her suitcase. "You know that it's better *this* way, right? Not like before when families lasted forever. Less nepotism." She was lying, just as she always did, because she didn't have the spine.

Zoðr puffed ler cheeks full of air and popped ler lips open. Keð dropped it. They couldn't start fighting about politics on day one.

Bhamsă made blunt comments about Maðzi culture in that exact same way, albeit *privately* disagreeing with official policy. Keð and Tantas had gone after people with similar personalities. Moreover, Zoðr was an atan. Bhamsă was a tănda. Similar.

Keð wished that she had said something much more meaningful than, *I miss you*, in that final text.

The robot found Keð's luggage. The hover-tech didn't start on the first or second try, so the robot kicked it repeatedly. It whirred to life with a sputter. Keð held back a chuckle. She was too tired. It wouldn't do to look chipper or the family wouldn't let her sleep.

"Thank you," Keð said to the service robot. The hover-tech on the left side rocked like it would give up again.

"You're welcome," it said. The synthflesh face looked too human when it smiled. Keð quickly looked away.

CHAPTER TWO

THE SINÅMN HOUSE had already decorated for the holiday. Retinal-purple, leafy wreaths adorned every door. Two storage crates of fuchsia streamers lay out on the dining table benches, and the household robot ironed them in patient silence to prepare for hanging them from the ceilings and across the windows.

The traditional ancestor offerings of dry-roasted nuts and seeds lay in three artisanal bowls on the house's main shrine. The bowls' sides wove together in sharp, mathematically-rich geometries, purple mingling with white and black, each a unique display of talent at carving wood, stone, and bone. Keð paused to stare. She and Tantas hadn't grown up in wealth. The bowls in the Qamalin ancestral home were made of plain steel and obsidian, fitting for a conservative family that still held fast to the anti-ostentation teachings of the zěbank philosophers.

This new house had five obsidian-carved statues that stood half a meter tall, abstract icons with only the barest impressions of noses and hair. Each had its hands spread out. It was impossible to render hair without showing gender. Qamalin had wood-carved ancestor statues and decorative photographs. This new household

14

was so different that Keð wondered if she should say anything at all. She felt like such a tourist, gawking, like the ones she and Tantas had made fun of as kids in their home village.

"Keð," Tantas said.

She looked up. Zoðr and Tantas were standing at the beginning of a short hallway, the former beckoning her to come. She felt like she was floating, just like the suitcase, she was so fatigued.

The guest room was small and looked out onto the back garden. She set her luggage down, turned off her suitcase, and walked to the bench of plants by the window to look out. Every Mamlt household grew traditional greens. In the tropics, the year went from wet to dry and back again with a familiar pattern of vegetation. The remains of the dry-season garden hung drying just above her head. The garden would be beautiful later in spring.

"The larger guest room is Zoðr's greenhouse," Tantas said apologetically. "Hey, you okay?"

"It smells nice," Keð said. "My compliments."

Zoðr met her eyes again and cleared ler throat. "We'll let you settle in? We're making a late dinner, if you're up for it."

"Yes." Keð twisted her torso towards the bed and glanced down at the duvet's intricate, flowing patterns. More ostentation. "I'll let you know if I need anything. Food — food sounds nice."

They ate pounded winter pancakes flecked with green and red from the herbs and spices. The sizzling grilled meat and creamy, fatty ðu̩tl fruit felt happy and whole in Keð's gut. Fresh ðu̩tl never survived the journey to Dukkă on the train.

Beyond Zoðr, Tantas, and Qentas, Keð met a man with her own name and a woman, Qasen, who'd joined the sinåmn house a year after its founding. The family drilled Keð with so many questions that it was a relief to get away and go back to the guest room. She stared out at the dark garden filled with the bones of dead plants, all in shadow. When she closed her eyes, she could still feel the movement of the train.

Keð fell asleep fast and awoke at predawn when her tablet pinged.

It was another message from Bhamsă. *Let's meet in ten days by the Red Temple, near the forest path.* Keð responded *yes* and lay back down in bed, staring at the ceiling. It would be nice to see lim.

The house was silent. Sleep wouldn't come. She pushed away the covers and put on a house coat. The patterns glowed slightly in the darkness. Keð frowned down at them and went out into the darkness of the hallway towards the living room.

The utility robot sat charging against a wall, a soft light breathing orange behind its head. The ancestor shrine lay deep in shadow.

It was a reasonable enough hour to have something hot to drink. Keð fumbled with a hot water kettle in the kitchen and set it to boil. She searched through the label-free cupboards for qumsa and tisanes. It was a well-stocked kitchen, with festival cakes in food preservation drawers, half-fermented bean pastes and winter vegetables in neat stacks in a crisper, and well-labeled jars of flours. Dry-season vegetables preserved in salt sat in the one place Keð anticipated finding tisanes, a lone rotten ðụtl fruit in front of them. Keð threw it out.

The household's instant qumsa was not in a programmed food preservation unit, but in a thin cupboard beside the sink, tucked behind other instant tisanes, loose leaf teas, and spices. There was even loose qumsa, a mix of the plant's small seeds and leaves, in a transparent glass jar.

Keð didn't want to rattle around through the pots and pans to find the vessel to boil the loose qumsa. She waited for the kettle to finish boiling and mixed in the powder. It smelled a bit old, but dissolved easily. She set it down on the kitchen counter and slipped past the island, bound for the bookcase along the far wall of the open room.

The bookcase was half-full, with children's books set in a neat pile on the bottom shelf, each wrapped with a single blue cord to signify that they were gifts. The shelf at shoulder height was messy. She picked out an anthology of memorial poems, grooved in one place by a crease, and read the first few lines of the marked poem before closing the book to bring back with her to read at the table. She sat down with her quṃsa and opened to the first page. It began with mudslide memorials, which she flipped past without reading. The book landed on the marked poem again, its binding primed.

A door clicked open in the hallway. Keð closed the book. Tantas emerged from the hallway, sleep-mussed hair emerging from her head like solar prominences, almost the color of an H-α emission image.

Tantas slipped onto the bench across from Keð and rested her head against her fists. "You're up."

Keð grimaced. "I know."

"You were quiet yesterday," Tantas said. She lowered her arms and yawned. "That's not like you."

Keð closed the book and pushed it aside. She sighed and mumbled, "I was tired."

"What do you think of the family?"

"They're fine." Keð flinched as Tantas reached over to grab the book. "Zoðr is trying too hard. I don't disapprove of the marriage. You're fine."

Tantas frowned. She opened up right to the bookmarked page. "I tried explaining to Iim and the others what it means to have a sister in the BC. It didn't work very well. So much of what you do is classified that I couldn't even explain it. It makes things really difficult."

Keð sipped her quṃsa. "I can't give you classified information just to make them happy. What's the poem?"

"We're planning to read it during the ancestor rites," Tantas said softly.

"You're a good reader." Keð smiled and slipped off of the bench. She warmed up more water and pulled more instant quṃsa out of the cabinet. "You're doing that even with the—"

"I'm barely pregnant. Lilinbaðu won't notice."

"Could you read it to me?"

Tantas cleared her throat. The rich cadence of Tantas' Mamltab could have landed her a career in performance art, secular or religious, but she'd chosen to follow Keð's career path as closely as a civilian could by joining the community police force. It had robbed the world of a talented recitation artist.

> *Zakl blam wụmibo teðqawo.*
> *Eton cilob xamb ðranten br zakl,*
> *ğako zakl zotib mo ċiqe ebam.*

> *Oneb talðr sawenċron eniwo.*
> *Ğako mo asr nam osụ blsa cimamoz zakl,*
> *babim ğim zeb kimomibo lilintas mansam.*

> You were buried in the forest.
> I placed you among yellow br,
> which the short disease starved you from.

> With us, grief was not anchorable.
> These folds of red fabric remember you,
> waves that trace out death's language.

When Tantas stopped reading, she set the closed book back on the table. Keð couldn't recite nearly as well and hadn't at any of the festivals after she was ten or eleven.

"I'm going to wake the robot. The others will want breakfast soon. Are you going to be with us today?" Tantas asked.

Keð shook her head. "I'm going to a restaurant while everything's still open."

"Okay. We were planning to visit the market for some last-minute things." Tantas smiled. "Transit should be better this holiday. The metro line to our parents' home just opened if you want to do the ancestor ritual with them."

Their parents lived a thirty or forty minute walk away, a distance easily managed by someone in active service. "Yeah, it's my duty to be there."

It was Tantas' turn to look down and get uncomfortable. Keð had known their womb-mother, grandparents, and extended family better than Tantas. Still, both had seen those faces on the ancestor shrine growing up, the smart-animated photographs turning their heads or laughing together as if alive. Their oğam-parent usually cried at some point while reading the prepared ancestral passages and poems.

It wasn't a good time to fight. Keð said, "I didn't mean it like you think — just that I should be there."

Tantas wiped tears from her eyes and murmured, "Zoðr has a contact in an apartment along the parade route tonight. We'll be there, not watching with you all."

The ancestor rites happened just after sunset, and the parade happened two hours before midnight.

Every year, the goddess' statue was carried from the sacred precinct at the Temple of the Multitudes to the goddess' sacred grove of red linðo trees. It went along two of the major Asraqan roads. There was a small window of time to seek the icon's blessing. Once installed in Lilinbaðu̞'s sacred grove, the statue would reside there while the dead walked the earth in the cities and towns of Mamltaqal. When it returned, they left for another year.

Keð was old enough now to know that memories of the dead lingered long after their spirits descended into the underworld again, trapped in the shadows of others' glances and the hushed whispers of well-meaning, clumsy bystanders. The memory of Wiren still caused an ache in her chest.

"What time are you leaving?"

"After breakfast."

Keð nodded. She chugged the remainder of her qumsa and returned the book to its shelf. Tantas left the kitchen area and walked to the robot to activate it.

When the household appliance whirred to life, its limbs clicked stiffly. It came into a standing position — not as graceful as a killer Sentinel, but a mechanical presence all the same. People preferred it when their utility robots made noise so they knew when they were there. A robot didn't breathe.

It bowed slightly before following Tantas to the kitchen.

Keð left for her room. She rummaged through her things until she found the photo of Wiren, printed from Keð's archive of mementos at the school in Asraqan. She'd go directly from the restaurants and downtown shopping to her parents' house, she decided.

The two had few photos from their years of service, so this one came from their late teens, just before the curriculum had become hard and practical. Keð looked a lot more like her younger self than Wiren did. Wiren had lost a lot of weight in the near-decade since, and she'd stopped eating regularly a few months before her death. Keð hadn't noticed the festering silence growing between them until the very end.

Wiren had always asked too many questions. Why communications in the civilian sector had to be tethered. Why BC alone had authorization to use a limited band of radio frequencies with high deterioration rates so they wouldn't reach beyond Maðz's solar system. What the probability *actually* was that hostile aliens would rip their way into a sector of space that had human voices and images instead of the silence between stars. If Keð had noticed something was wrong and told Bhamsă, maybe things would have been different — Wiren reassigned to a less stressful job, not put out in the countryside to decommission an illegal spacecraft.

Keð put the photograph in her day purse and closed her eyes. She cleared her mind just as her trainers had taught, making it smooth as glass, like the Mamltab language.

Besides, Lilinbaðų hadn't left yet. Wiren had no power to return and blame Keð when she was trapped in the underworld and Keð properly observed the sacred rites to keep her tame.

CHAPTER THREE

KEÐ AND HER parents found a spot along the parade route not far from the BC school. They heard the procession long before they saw it. A band played somber, major scale laments while two men on a float sang discordant, intentionally tuneless hymns. It sounded like wailing at the funerary rites. By the time the band reached them, its singers were sweaty, voices half-spent.

Behind the float, sixteen teenage girls and oğam carried festival baskets on their heads made of dried, blackened twigs and leaves. Each festival basket contained raw br grain with a knife hidden at the bottom. The grain symbolized life and fertility and potential — the knife, death. Only twins who had lost a sibling marched.

One youth among the sixteen would be mock-sacrificed and replaced with an animal at the last moment, following the ritual story of how Lilinbaðu came to Asraqan. The sacrificial animal, a black-furred ćiza, followed. Its coiling neck swayed to take in the crowd on either side.

The crowd roared and cheered as the goddess' statue made its way down the wide boulevard behind the procession. Photographs gleamed in the lamplight as they struck it.

Keð sucked her tongue against the inside of her upper front teeth, her stomach suddenly doing flip-flops. Her hands shook as she searched for Wiren's photograph in her left pocket. It was in her right. She took it out and tried not to hold her breath.

Her father squeezed her shoulder.

Mamlt women weren't supposed to show stress like this in public. Keð had not become an atan or a ximsa. She followed orders and showed emotions easily — it didn't matter in Dukkă, but now in Asraqan, she was just as self-conscious as she had been growing up, when other children teased her for acting like an oğam. Girls represented steadfastness, family values, and mental alacrity. Oğam were the mediators of birth, and so they stood for the empathy, hard work, and nurturing qualities it took to be the emotional anchors for their families.

Her oğam-parent whispered, "It would be best if you didn't glare at the goddess."

Keð stopped gritting her teeth. She reached back and grabbed her oğam-parent's hand. It was warm. Le pulled her close. Keð's fist fell awkwardly to her side, crushing Wiren's photograph against her bell-embellished pants.

She closed her eyes and said a prayer. As the statue passed, she flung Wiren's image towards it. It landed just short of Lilinbaðų's feet. The atan religious officiant accompanying the goddess' statue cleared the photograph away with all of the others to be offered in the grove fire pit.

Her parents had decades of practice throwing the myriad photographs of their dead relatives. Her father handed Keð four — they took care of the others. Keð hadn't helped throw them until the third year after the mudslide, when she was old enough for them to trust her aim.

Keð's earliest memories of Sentinels weren't as killing machines, but as saviors who had dug her out of a partially-collapsed building after a day with no water. It had been difficult to talk to Wiren about the accident — impossible to bring up to Vait, who wouldn't understand how it made her family bonds stronger.

Wiren's family doubtless stood in a festival like this at 29th parallel, throwing their own images. At 29th parallel, however, they didn't bring their goddess of death through the city.

Keð tried to banish Wiren from her mind.

After Lilinbaðu passed, the three returned to her childhood home. Her oğam-parent opened a bottle of greenish-amber alcohol while her father made steamed sticky cakes bathed in spicy red oil. They talked late into the night about everything but Keð's job — mostly Keð's womb-mother. It was a night of remembering some dead, forgetting others.

Keð and her sister had an old room upstairs, now rented out to university students during the term. No one would be boarding now. She considered asking to stay, but nothing but the sheets would be the same. She decided that she felt sober enough to walk home.

It was silent outside. The new train line rumbled nearby, although she couldn't see it through the houses and trees, and she followed it until she reached one of the boulevards. More people were outside, along with robots and utility androids. Keð stopped to monitor a drunken brawl between two brothers until a robotic peacekeeper arrived to fume both with tranquilizers and register them. She continued on to a shortcut to Tantas' house, a path through Waba Park.

There, the wind picked up. It cast deep, roping shadows along the ground. Keð pulled up her collar and drew her scarf hard around the lower part of her face. Few walked in Asraqan's parks this late at night while the dead roamed, but the overlook view always took her breath away. She stayed there for a while before she moved on towards the hilly district where her sister lived.

Zoðr let Keð into the house. A wide bowl of tisane warmed on the kitchen stove, tendrils of steam coiling in front of the windows. Zoðr ladled some for Keð and brought her into the living room. She wasn't in the mood to socialize, but it would be rude to just go to bed.

Tantas thunked her hand on the couch seat beside her and yelled, "Hey storm cloud, come and sit down with us!"

Keð smiled into her tisane as she took a sip. She mock-frowned as she walked over and said, "I'm not the one making the thunder."

Still, she curled into a sitting position. The utility robot knelt between the two couches and started to set up a verse game that Keð had never excelled at. She was better at noticing good poetry than reciting it on her own.

They played for about an hour before everyone drifted off to their beds. The tisane made Keð groggy-wired. In the guest room, she pulled the blankets up to her throat, snuggling in. There was a draft from the window.

That night, Keð's dreams started fitfully, focusing first on an imaginary grandparent's skeleton in a box covered in claw marks that looked like mountain peaks. It was as if the purificatory rituals had never happened, that Lilinbaðu had not been satisfied.

Somehow, in the dream, the photograph that had caused this was not the grandparent — it was Wiren. The photograph of her friend had looked so unlike the Wiren who had died that it was impossible for the ghost to recognize itself.

It must have been that, dream-Keð realized with horror.

Lilinbaðu, by now, had arrived at her sacred grove. Wiren was coming in through the back garden, leaving frost in her wake where her ghost-feet touched the weave-grass between the garden plots. The frigid air cracked open the stones that marked the path among the herbs. Water vapor frosted against Keð's window.

Wiren passed through the windowpanes without effort. She was all softness and smoke, barely a person, yet the cold sank through the spring-weight blankets and into Keð's bones. The spectral blood poured down Wiren's face and soaked into her uniform, and blood bubbled up through Wiren's lips when she attempted to speak. There was a bullet hole in her forehead. Keð knew this was a dream because it shouldn't have been there. It had been fire that killed Wiren, not metal.

Keð pulled the blankets closer, but it did nothing to stop the chill from spreading out and down. The mechanical clock on the empty bookshelf stopped ticking the seconds. Wiren snapped her fingers. The bones cracked. Blood dribbled from Wiren's chin onto the wood bed frame.

It didn't feel like a dream. Keð half expected someone from Dukkă to appear outside, perhaps Dispatcher Bhamsă limself. The violence in Keð's workplace had always *remained* at work, never penetrating into her dreams.

She dislodged her fingertips from the duvet and wormed them towards her tablet on the bedside table. Hooked into the house's system, it could do anything guest privileges allowed — turn on lights, start the oven, check the produce best-by dates — and now, Keð just wanted to have less darkness. Ghosts hated that.

As Keð unlocked the tablet, Wiren dove onto the bed, landing on her hands and knees. Keð screamed. The lights-off button was the last thing Keð had used before sleeping — she couldn't see to toggle it — and now the blood dripped onto her face. Did it mean anything if she swallowed it? As the ghost tried to flatten her down, Keð hammered her index finger against the tablet again. Nothing happened.

Wiren grabbed her wrists.

It was summer, and they were nineteen. It was the first day of spring leave. They raced through the school hallways as the rain came down outside and the other students fought with mud in the courtyard. The duo went hand-in-hand, their summer sandals slapping against the tiled floors.

Wiren saw the open door first and stopped. Keð skidded, pulled back by Wiren's steady grip. Instructor Ŭbhai's office, the astronomer nowhere to be seen. Keð's heart caught in her throat as Wiren glanced back and forth down the hall—

The lights rose. Keð was still screaming. She struggled against the grip that held her down. It was the other Keð, the man in Tantas' house. Tantas stood with a pitcher of ice water in the doorway.

"You can let go of me," Keð murmured. "I'm awake."

The other Keð let go. Tantas set the pitcher down on the empty bookshelf and came over to sit on the side of the bed. Keð searched through the room for her tablet. It lay face-down on the floor, saved from shattering by engineering and its hardy, military-grade case.

The bed's swirling indigo and pink designs had some dried soil on them, perhaps tracked in from the garden. Keð saw no blood.

"What are you looking for?" Tantas asked. "Are you sure I don't need the pitcher?"

"The duvet's dirty," Keð murmured.

The other Keð said, "Zoðr didn't clean the duvet?"

Tantas sighed. "That atan." She examined the duvet and sucked her tongue against her teeth. "We can get you another duvet cover. They're in the hall closet."

"I really think we should tell Zoðr to keep the plants to the big guest room. We need a place to entertain. We can't have herbs *everywhere*," the other Keð said. Keð had to agree.

It was barely dawn outside, the sky paling to clear. Keð untangled herself from the sheets and came into a cross-legged position. She waited while Tantas fetched the other cover. Tantas and other-Keð changed the duvet while Keð watched, her eyes slightly unfocused. She had never had a nightmare like this before. The world still felt unreal around its edges.

Lilinbaðų had a retinue of the dead, Keð thought, and a goddess of death might know that Keð was sleeping with her demimortal boss, a member of the acimta collective mind. Joining one of those collectives was like a snub against goddesses like that. What if they bore grudges against the living whom people like Bhamsă fucked? There were, after all, stories. Or — that sounded wrong. Her therapist would have called it reaching too far. Maybe it wasn't even about Wiren, ultimately. Maybe it was Vait's fault.

"You've got that look again," Tantas said. She threw the duvet at Keð, who blinked when it hit her in the face.

The other Keð tucked the lightweight duvet into the base of the bed. This one was yellow, with vines that wove through in red, green, and violet, also animated. Tantas had changed so much if she now allowed such loud patterns into her home. It must have been one of the others in the sinåmn house, a person less tied to the zebånk tradition.

"Nothing, just thinking," Keð said.

Tantas sighed. "Are you going to be okay? Do you want the robot here?"

"Does the robot have a name?" Keð asked.

The other Keð sucked in air through his teeth. Tantas clenched her jaw. It was a new robot in a sinåmn house. It wouldn't have a name yet. Names came after a robot's first few years, once it developed a semi-human personality and learned how to live with its family — unless it was a binma, a robot with a human personality layer. Binma were legally people, and they couldn't be bought. The dig was uncalled for, but so was Wiren stalking into the house like a death-demon bent on sucking Keð into the earth.

Slowly, Keð relaxed into the bed. She fluffed the pillows and held out one hand to her sister, whose eyes welled as if she might cry. "Hey, I didn't mean it."

Tantas blinked. Two tears fell down her cheeks. She breathed in sharply. "It's not very lucky to hear that with the pregnancy."

"I know."

Tantas grabbed Keð's hand. Keð pulled her down into the bed and held her close. This sinåmn-married Tantas used the same shampoo as the Tantas Keð had known growing up, scented like flowers and the peppery cooking spices of late autumn. She stroked Tantas' hair and kissed her cheek once.

"I had a friend who died in service last year," Keð said as Tantas drew back. "Wiren. Do you remember her?"

Tantas' eyes widened. "The short girl from 29th?"

"Yeah."

"This is your first festival for Lilinbaðu after that, right?"

"Yeah. They don't do death the same way in Sò Gǎn. Dukkǎ, the big city, has something that only lasts a day or two." Everything still felt cold, as if someone had replaced Keð's bones with carved ice.

Keð kept her eyes on her sister, not on the man with her name. Tantas' gaze fell to the ground. She probably knew next to nothing about Sò Gǎn, Keð realized, and looking it up on the tablet *now* would be too conspicuous. Keð might have cared a year ago, but not now.

"You should go get an amulet blessed tomorrow," Tantas said. "Keep the ghost away, burn it after the festival when it can't come back."

It, Keð thought. "Yeah."

"We'll send in the robot to watch you sleep."

"Okay."

Keð turned the light off from her tablet when the two left. The robot took a cross-legged position between the bed and the wide window doors. Keð turned away from it. Her heart hammered, and sleep would not come easily. She turned back towards the robot. Even if she couldn't sleep, it would be good for her to see it.

The herbs on the bench along the wide windowsills were crushed right where Wiren had come through, their leaves blackened. That was how Keð knew that Wiren's apparition had been more than just a bad dream. Dreams didn't do *this*.

CHAPTER FOUR

KEÐ SLEPT IN until noon. The robot warmed leftovers for her in the kitchen while she did her bodyweight exercises, showered, and dressed. A note on Keð's tablet from Tantas said that they'd gone to a cleansing spring before it got busy later in the day. There was a hardly-readable scribble below from one of the others — *hope you're feeling more at ease*. She wasn't, and she wished that they had waited.

While she ate, she tethered in and examined the festival register. She and her parents had a shared calendar item for the next day, when they would cleanse themselves in the ocean, but the dream felt like scum against her skin, and she wanted something now. None of the sacred baths and overflow sites had space until that evening, and only then halfway across the city. It would have to wait.

The thought about finding a specialist popped into her head just as she'd finished. Spirit-workers who talked to the dead set up tents along the city's main boulevard. It wasn't exactly a purification, but she could book time.

Almost everyone was booked solid. She checked someone's profile who had a few spots left, and by the time she'd finished, the calendar was all red. The second person she found with slots, someone named Zebr, she booked quickly. *Zebr* was a traditionalist name — a good sign; it meant *treading lightly* and came from the same root as *zebånk*. She wouldn't be comfortable with someone from the new *iwånk* cultural movement, and she hoped for her ancestors' sakes that le wouldn't use plastic in ler charms. It was forbidden in *zebånk*, and the haunting might get worse.

The appointment time barely gave Keð enough time to check her travel route and close up the house. The city bustled with activity — impromptu masked rituals in its neighborhoods in front of popup shrines to Lilinbaðu or any number of the regional deities connected to the underworld or apotropaic rites. Asraqan held five million people, with families from all over the country and beyond. This was something she had missed in Dukkă.

She boarded a train headed for the city center. Many families crammed in with offerings for their families' grave sites in the small necropoles between city districts, so it was standing room only. In the city center, a crowd of teenagers was playing with water balloons in front of a purification temple for Đawiza just beyond the station. Since the god's temple was shut on underworld days, Keð decided they'd been filled with water filled from the lustral taps. It was hopelessly *iwånk*.

Keð joined the clusters of people wearing somber indigos, whites, grays, and dark reds who moved quickly among the spirit-workers' tents. The Rite of Cutting would begin at sunset in the amphitheater several blocks away, a ticketed affair simulcast on screens throughout the city, so the crowd would let up soon. People who could bear children could not attend the rite, so Keð was free until the offerings at midnight.

Each spirit-worker's tent was marked with the occupant's full name and spirit-worker license on the tent flap. Zebr was about halfway down the row. She stopped at a vendor stall for hot steamed cakes in meat sauce, and she ate them on a bench while she waited. The meeting time came and went, and still the tent was closed — *occupied*, with screams, yells, and metallic rattles coming from inside at intervals. She licked her fingers.

The client finally exited, a ximsa person with a small child in tow. Zebr waited at the doorway for the pair to leave. Keð put her trash in a bin and scrambled into the tent after him.

Sacred texts in a bookshelf lined one of the tent walls, components of charms in a crafting area along another, and a seating area in the center. Zebr was a man in his late fifties or early sixties, with medium-brown skin, hazel eyes, and verses tattooed on his forehead, face wizened with wrinkles. She would have preferred a ximsa. Gender renunciants had an easier connection to the spirit world, only slightly better than women.

Keð had already transferred funds for this, though, so she greeted Zebr and sat down across from him. Zebr took up the blackish indigo oracle spines and shook them.

"Hold out your hands. About shoulder-width," he said.

Keð did. Zebr let the oracle spines fall onto the square cloth between Keð's hands and studied the chaotic pattern they made along the grid.

"You saw a ghost in a dream that may have actually been a manifestation?" Zebr asked. His brow furrowed, and he put his index finger to his lips. "That's what you said in the appointment request."

"Yes."

The spirit-worker cleared his throat. "I see."

"Is something wrong?" Keð couldn't have interpreted the pattern without training.

Zebr looked up at her and frowned. He steepled his hands against his sternum. "Are you sure that this person is actually dead?"

"Of corse she is. There was a funeral. I was there."

The spirit-worker sighed. "The pattern is strange. It's not like a ghost. It seems to indicate a deity is involved. The wards I know against the dead might work, but they might not. I'll have to give you something strong. You should pray in a temple after they reopen."

"Does it say which goddess?"

"Not Lilinbaðụ. There are many gods who send the dead," Zebr said. He rose to his feet and went around Keð.

Glasses clinked. Keð listened as he put together the charm without saying a word. She was disappointed, but he *was* right — there were so many gods in the Mamlt pantheon, and even the same ones could be interpreted differently depending on the region. Wiren should have fallen under Lilinbaðụ's domain.

"What does 'a deity is involved' mean? *Could* it mean, I mean." The crunch of the pestle against the mortar reminded her of the sound Wiren had made.

Zebr sighed. "It means that the deity may not care about the rules of engagement for the living and the dead. I'm giving you some of the strongest warding herbs I possess. We'll bless them with a chant. You can burn this in a bonfire at the festival's end. Have a purification immediately after." He paused. "You're not thinking about going to mountains, are you?"

"My sister and I are going on a trip soon."

Zebr snapped his fingers. "The pattern on the ground indicates that mountains are involved in this — see the spines marked with the symbols for earth-and-sky and how they meet. It could be Amnðemn or Aċeðe. Then again, it could be a pastoral god, or one of roadways. Who knows? I would pray to everyone."

"Wiren didn't die in the mountains." Keð twisted her torso to face Zebr. She recalled what she had said to Vait a day earlier, that she was afraid of the mountain goddess —

"This should fix your problem, but be careful on that trip." He passed a glass vial over a candle and met Keð's eyes. His expression was almost sullen, as if Keð would correct herself and say that Wiren had died in mountains at any moment.

No wonder he had free slots, Keð thought.

Zebr blew out the candle and said, "And now we will chant. It's not important that you know what it means."

The chant was in Old Mamltab, the language once shared between Mamltaqal and Kotakl, preserved primarily in sacred texts. Keð repeated each line after him. It calmed her mind at the very least. She had serious questions about whether special power lay in dead languages. Mamltab would have sufficed if Zebr weren't partially doing this for show during a festival. Old Mamltab was eyebrow-raising even for hardcore traditionalists in cities like Asraqan.

When the chanting ended, Zebr sealed the vial and threaded cord through its lid. He tied it around Keð's neck. The air felt clearer, as if a weight had flown from Keð's chest through the air to land at Lilinbaðų's deathless feet.

Keð did not dream about Wiren that night or the nights after. At the close of the festival, two days before she and Tantas left for Qoziðamn, Keð burned it in a bonfire and breathed in the heavy smoke as it traveled up into the sliver of atmosphered sky.

CHAPTER FIVE

AFTER THE FESTIVAL ended, Keð donned white robes and took a train at midday to the Red Temple to see Bhamsă. It was only packed until she reached the edge of the business district, when she was finally able to sit down.

Asraqan had only ever been significant due to this temple complex, which sprawled across the largest of the sloping hills that encircled the bay. It was sacred to the goddess Momaqimnam, although shrines and smaller temples to about seventy other gods occupied the slopes. Momaqimnam had eight temple buildings and shrines, two monasteries, and an incubation facility.

Keð purified her hands and hair with ash when she arrived. She prayed briefly to the goddess at the first of her eight shrines, which lay just inside the sacred structure. She didn't have enough time to pray to *every* god here on the way up to the main temple, but she could at least honor the goddess of the place and whichever other gods caught her eye.

She spent the most time at Bamonkam and Samaðrem's shrines, which were really just small stone nooks grafted onto Momaqimnam's fifth temple structure. Keð had a small icon to

Bamonkam in her dormitory room back in Dukkă — he was a protective deity, here depicted sitting on a cloud while the winds raged below. Samaðrem had been Wiren's favorite. She'd been given Wiren's icon, but hadn't ever prayed to lim and did not even know any of ler myths. The mountain goddess, Amnðem, had a shrine right beside them. Keð lit incense there and said nothing, avoiding eye contact. She would be in the mountains so soon. There was no avoiding Amnðem there.

By the time she arrived at the temple's pilgrimage center, Bhamsă was already sitting in the open canteen. Everyone was dressed in white, required of temple visitors, or the green-and-brown robes of the ascetics and monastics.

Bhamsă was the only acim there — the name of the demimortal collective that le belonged to — and like all acim, Bhamsă's hair was white, ler skin pigmentless. It made lim invisible in the crowd until le stood up and waved at Keð.

Keð waited in the canteen line for temple food behind two monastics. An ascetic scooped porridge into a bowl for Keð and topped it with a bright green sauce, crunchy dried vegetables, and thin-cut strips of a dried sea animal called *uwecel*, one of three vegetative animals that were allowed in the temple diet. She took a sip of her drink before sitting down. It was astringent, and she wished that she'd known to water it down.

Bhamsă was already half-done with ler food by the time Keð reached lim. Keð bowed slightly and said, "Dispatcher, may I sit?"

"Go ahead," Bhamsă said.

Keð worked her way onto the bench and took two bites of her meal. When she swallowed, she said, "It's less hard than I thought it would be to come back."

Bhamsă set down ler spoon. Ler gaze unfocused for a moment, and when le looked at Keð again, le said, "You've kept up a good performance record despite a lot of hardship. Of course you'd be fine. How was the festival?"

"I'm staying at my sister's," Keð said. "It's strange. Did you know that she and Zoðr went sinåmn? It wasn't what they said they'd do."

Her Dispatcher smiled and pushed ler bowl aside to make room for ler hands to fidget. Bhamsă started to speak twice, not going farther than *I*. At last, le sighed and said, "It was known to me that your sister didn't share some things with you. You didn't tell her anything about what happened after Wiren died — your medical leave, for instance. You lied to her. I remember advising against that?"

Keð took a mouthful of porridge. The cooking water came from the sacred springs, so it was important to eat the entire meal, but she didn't have an appetite. Keð would have preferred to never hear about the medical leave again — the insomnia after Wiren's funeral that had pushed her over the breaking point and the forced recuperation time that had taken the prior year's entire leave allotment, all of the months of therapy and stress checks ever since. Medical records were things that people like Vait could see in the private version of her profile if they broke decorum, but the BC's analysis of Keð was something that not even *she* could see because it was above-clearance. She didn't want to give any of her fellow officers more than what they had in the data.

She decided not to speak directly to Bhamsă's point. Keð hadn't been thinking clearly after the tragedy, and now she had to live with every embarrassing, stressful outcome of what she'd done afterward. "Vait was trying to bait me on the train."

"Not surprising. Vait works better alone than with people," Bhamsă said. "He's good at finding vulnerabilities and prodding at them, just like how you're good at going into a situation and keeping the body count low. We put each of you where your style was most useful."

Keð downed the rest of her drink in one go. She cleared her throat and said, "He says he likes me."

"He says that about everyone."

"How are your rounds going? Are you taking—"

"It's just a pretense," Bhamsă said. "It barely takes any time to review new people, perhaps about fifteen hours of work each week. I am recharging. There are friends at Acimtaxes whom I haven't seen in several years. We claim we'll have fun, but we all end up sleeping and complaining about people we know. I'm off to the next Academy in four days."

Acimtaxes was the seat of the acimta, located on another of Asraqan's hills. Keð had only ever seen one photograph — the one in the assembly hall of the Academy, with the leader of Maðz's acimta, Sawaho, smiling while standing on the front steps. There was another photograph of Elan, the leader of the other demimortal collective called the sazrim, perched on a climbing tree. Both groups staffed the upper echelons of the BC with people like Bhamsă. Keð had seen the inside of Elan's headquarters because it was in Dukkă, and Elan hosted a reception for BC officers. Bhamsă's acim status sometimes made Keð anxious. She had never felt that way about a sazr.

"What kind of fun?"

"We were going to rent a boat and take it out on the bay, but it's been a bit choppy," le said. "Eat up. I want to go to the temple. Are you free for the rest of the day? You could come with me."

Keð said, "My parents and I are having dinner later."

"Hours from now." Bhamsă smiled. "Good."

They ate quickly and washed their bowls at the edge of the canteen. Beyond that lay one of the monasteries, just at the foot of the stone steps up to Momaqimnam's temple. Purple streamers billowed from strong lampposts, and all of the trees on this hill's summit were fuchsia-leaved with retinal.

Momaqimnam's doors were open. She and Bhamsă switched from shoes into thin white slippers, joining the goddess' prostration line. Keð folded her arms across her chest and shifted her weight from foot to foot, gaze landing on the murals around them, seeing them and not seeing them. Being back in Asraqan and visiting its temples was a lot like seeing an old home after a series of new owners. She was so used to ritual in Dukkǎ — decentralized, with only itinerant officiants, where even someone's bedroom could be made into a ritual site with the correct knowledge.

Her gaze rested on a scene of Momaqimnam with Amnðem, the sisters locked in conflict with each other. Momaqimnam had ensnared Amnðem with a net, yet Amnðem could still shoot her poison darts through it. *The wilderness is always victorious, and all we have is a gift from Momaqimnam*, the teaching went.

They maintained religious silence throughout. Keð prostrated before Momaqimnam nine times before she breathed powdered incense onto the goddess' fire while making eye contact with the icon, a piece of sandstone carved in the shape of a young woman. She left via the side door to receive a priestess's blessing — sap on her lips from Momaqimnam's trees — and waited outside under a grove of trees for Bhamsǎ to emerge.

A first touch happened between them there. Bhamsǎ brushed sap from Keð's cheek and licked it from ler finger absently, a soft smile on ler face. And then le *was* blushing. Keð wanted to kiss lim. She stood frozen.

"Do you want to go anywhere else?" Bhamsǎ asked.

"I've seen the shrines I needed," Keð said. "Where do you want to go?"

Bhamsǎ beckoned.

They descended the hill on the train together and switched to another line on the outskirts of Asraqan, which they rode for two stops before switching trains. Keð knew deep down that they were bound for the house of the acim, Acimtaxes, and the thought made her stomach churn. She wanted to say *not there*, but what was she to do, contradict her Dispatcher?

It wasn't like having sex in the acim's local house in Dukkǎ. Acimtaxes was an official place — almost sacred.

The forest path from the train was serene and silent save the cries of animals. Its Sentinel guardians, hidden just out of view, could be lurking in decoy trees. She kept her spine straight, almost at military attention. The forest path soon gave way to gardens and arbors. Anywhere else, Keð would have stopped to look. Bhamsǎ's pace was a near-march.

Nobody stopped either of them at the door. They removed their shoes and walked down a narrow side hallway until they arrived at Bhamsǎ's room. Keð's stomach churned every time they passed someone. Everyone in the acimta knew about the two of them because the acimta could have no secrets. This was as much a display of power for Bhamsǎ as it was about just having sex.

They disrobed by the door and folded their clothes neatly. Bhamsǎ said, "You can shower before you leave. It's a communal stall down the hall, much like what you're used to."

Keð nodded once.

Bhamsǎ's window looked out onto one of the inner gardens. She sat on the edge of the bed and watched nesting birds in the tree just outside until Bhamsǎ came to sit beside her.

"You're not at ease," le said.

"We could have picked a hotel. Acimtaxes is weird."

Bhamsǎ shrugged. Le stroked one hand down Keð's back, leaving goosebumps in ler fingers' wake. Perhaps the questions were not so important now. Bhamsǎ pressed Keð down onto the bed, chest to chest, the nipples on their breasts touching. Ler hands gripped her wrists firmly. Keð kept from giggling by looking up into Bhamsǎ's eyes — so, so pale, and so, so beautiful.

Afterward, Keð lay in the bed staring up at the ceiling. She'd thought of a poem near climax, something she'd found in the library at the Academy when she was sixteen or so, a piece that she and Wiren had read aloud together.

Most of the memory lay in shadow, but the sliding door of this small room and the simple traditionalism of Acimtaxes' decor called up something about lovers lingering long because heartbreak lay at the door.

Bhamsă had to walk Keð back to the train. This time, they passed a common room, and she felt the stares of all of the people there at her back.

CHAPTER SIX

THE TRAIN TO Qoziðamn left the following afternoon, and it stopped at each transit hub that took trains cross-longitude — a much longer ride than the route that Keð had taken to Asraqan. As the sun set, the picturesque foothills and sleepy villages were swallowed up in the blackness, as if a great inkwell had overturned to coat the world. The smooth tracks stood still in a starless expanse of space. Her reflection stared back at her in the glass.

Many hours later, they reached Krta at 34th parallel, its capped lights visible even as the train bowed its head down into the valley. They transferred at Akrtan, the next stop, and headed east along the 38th parallel transit artery.

Keð slept in fits and starts. She awoke at midmorning to read the guidebook for Qoziðamn on her tablet, mindful of each station as it passed.

Qoziðamn skirted the edge of Mamltaqal's most productive higher-lat farmland due to its rich volcanic soils. It would have photogenic scenes — lakes in extinct and dormant calderas, gorges, cliffs — all ready for hiking. The floor plan for their one-bedroom rental seemed spacious enough to hold both of them if the reconciliation gambit failed.

There wasn't a tether point between Akrtan and their destination, and they must have passed one in the middle of the night while they slept. The train's emptiness felt eerie, and her gut clenched. It wasn't right.

They reached Qoziðamn in the early afternoon and detrained quickly with their luggage. It was only several degrees above freezing. Tantas shivered from the cold, and Keð gave her a scarf.

The village's tourist block sat sleepily at the edge of town, where it overlooked terraces of farmland, karål pens, and quiet mountain streams. Rocky forests encircled the mountainous farmlands for kilometers.

A robot answered them when they reached the block manager's house. Keð and Tantas peered beyond it at the luncheon party in the main atrium. Nobody living noticed the two of them — they sat on their ground cushions so deep in discussion that Keð doubted they'd have heard even a fire alarm.

Tantas handled the robot more brusquely than Keð thought appropriate, but in the end, they received the key. Tantas continued to walk fast until they reached their place. She tried the key three times before asking Keð to help.

The key caught in the door when Keð tried turning it. She wiggled it until the door came open.

They set their luggage on the racks just within the door and kicked off their shoes. Tantas hit the lights, illuminating both the living area and kitchen. She ran to the bathroom.

"Almost full service, sans robots," Tantas said with a smile as she came out. "It's not like when Zoðr and I go camping."

"And they're really making this comfortable for Southerners," Keð widened her eyes to stay awake. She studied the low, cushioned couches clustered around the living area's Stream hookups and fought back a yawn.

Tantas' brow furrowed. "You don't like it?"

"No, I mean they'd have had to import this from around where you live." Keð sighed. "It's beautiful, Tantas."

Keð treaded lightly into the tiled open kitchen and to the bedroom at the left. The bedframe was extremely Southern, but without the swirling patterns carved into the wood like in Tantas' home. The bathroom had a perfumed oil and lotion dispenser just beside the soaps.

"Do we have dishes?" Keð asked. She looked back out into the kitchen as she worked lotion into her chapped hands.

Tantas shrugged and walked towards the cabinet above the induction plates. When she pulled it open, Keð took inventory as Tantas called out what was there: Three metal mixing bowls, a stainless steel pan, and a combination soup-steamer pot. The tiny convenience oven beside the induction burners held a small pan, and the storage area beneath contained an assortment of cutlery, cutting boards, tongs, and a scraper.

Keð said, "We could make dumplings stuffed with xlne."

Tantas checked the freezer and refrigerator. The former contained frozen qumsa pellets, perhaps left by the last guests. "These are still in date. Do we have a list?"

Keð left the bathroom doorway and leaned against the wall just by the stove. "It probably closes soon. We don't have time for that. What else do we need?"

"Flour, maybe some spices and nut milks? Meat. We need meat." Tantas reached into one of her pockets and started scribbling down a list with a pen. It leaked ink onto her fingers, but she kept writing. "Dried seaweeds. They won't have fresh here."

Keð walked past Tantas to take a better inventory of the cupboards. She located the register of cleaning services — laundry every other day placed in a bin at the front door, vacuuming and other robotic services every three days — and glanced around for her tablet to note down the times. It was still in the bag. Keð hadn't checked in with BC yet.

It could wait until after they got back.

The sisters left ten minutes later and took the winding pathway from their rental towards the village center. Sunlight licked through the terraces, catching the finest films of water.

Keð smiled and took her sister's hand. "It's really beautiful up here."

"Yeah," Tantas said. "Dad said that you'd like it. You're based in a city, right?"

"Mostly. We spend some time in back country, mostly places without Stream connections everywhere — it depends on the job. Lots of work in Sò Gǎn, sometimes across the border in Sò Hóta. It's not like here." Keð put her other hand in her pocket. The temperature would drop fast after sunset, and she couldn't wait to be in bed and sleeping.

"How far is the border from Dukkǎ?"

"Three hours on the train. We have a private van we use sometimes — six, seven hours driving."

They turned the corner into Qoziðamn's small downtown. A constellation of older adults played strategy games outside of a restaurant, breath catching like frost in the capped lighting as they gossiped.

A lot of BC officers retire to places like this, Keð thought, *if they don't die.*

The grocery store was busy. Staff, robots, and customers yelled at one another, words composed of an assortment of click consonants and vowels that sounded nearly like standard Mamltab, but not enough to be intelligible. The persistence of Amntaltab was startling. Everyone possessed a Stream connection, and Mamltaqal rarely broadcast content in regional languages.

The meat counter's customers waited shoulder-to-shoulder, all vying over cuts of red, pink, and purple-orange animal flesh wrapped in biodegradable seq material. Tantas pushed her way through the crowd and grabbed seven or eight prepackaged cuts, hands groping uncertainly in the rush. Tantas when *not* pregnant would have done the same thing, but the cuts of meat she grabbed were different — purple-orange u̩krsn, mostly deboned shoulders and back-arms, which held the most meat. Keð held out the basket. Tantas threw them in and immediately moved back into the crowd to find u̩krsn broth.

They picked up dough, flour, nut milk, and spices. Along the front of the store lay prepared food of all kinds. Keð stopped in front of the dumplings and gestured for Tantas to stop. The folded and shaped doughs contained everything from puffy tubers to meats and leafy vegetables. Keð's mouth watered. "Do you want dumplings tonight?"

"Yeah," Tantas said. "These look so fresh."

They bought nine packages.

At the checkout, a robotic attendant separated the prepackaged from by-weight items. The payment finished in seconds after a scan of Keð's ID card.

Keð had unlimited credits, which Tantas didn't know, as a perk of being a BC officer. Everything she purchased went into data tables.

The robotic attendant said, "You have three unread alerts, Keð Teðqawo Qamalin, one marked urgent."

"Guess we'd better head back," Tantas said. She stuck out her tongue as she lifted one of the bags. "You're just so important."

Keð rolled her eyes. "Shut up. I'm on vacation." She grabbed the other two bags. "Tantas, I can take that."

"No, I'm fine. Really."

"Are you sure?"

Tantas rolled her eyes.

The sisters set off behind a small family. Keð deliberately slowed down. Instead of taking a direct route, she led her sister along the road that wound straight through the town.

Qoziðamn had two temples, one to a mountain goddess syncretized with Amnðem. Her epithets streamed down the sides of the temple's outer walls in gold and obsidian. *She of Rock and Snow. Our Lady of Avalanches and Peaks. Forest-Shaker. Bird-Slayer. Dawn-*

Quaker. Obscurer. The only part that looked like a name was *Tltinðab*. The temple windows glowed with cozy light, and its chimney bellowed with lovely-scented smoke.

The other temple was for Momaqimnam. It lay quiet and undisturbed, future offerings of dried meat on pikes to the right and left of its doors.

Along the street side lay shrines to minor deities, candles slumping half-melted and still lit. A few villagers lingered in oblation, intoning hymns over offerings of small cakes and an opaque white liquid that Keð didn't recognize. All but the ximsa-gender worshippers kept their heads covered when they prayed. Neither Keð nor Tantas had thought to purchase offerings or a second scarf.

There was a definite tension in the villagers' eyes as the two passed. Keð noted it and filed it next to her anxiety about the alert.

Tantas shifted the bag to her other arm and said, "Do you think we should visit one of the temples after we're settled?"

"Maybe tomorrow." Keð made a show of shivering. "It's getting kind of cold, and I guess I have to check my tablet."

Those watchful, judgmental gazes meant that something had happened, and they had just missed it. The unknown event hung as palpable as thin paper streamers during Lilinbaðu̯'s festival. Qoziðamn was remote enough for two women to disappear, and Keð had no guns while off duty. She wasn't connected to Sentinels.

"Okay, that works. I want to check in with Zoðr when we get in, after we've put everything away," Tantas said, "along with everyone else."

"Like the other Keð?"

"Yeah." Tantas looked at her feet. "Look, you and I don't have to do this. I didn't *pick* someone with the same name as you. It wasn't like I wanted to replace sabtaza-you with some guy. We already had plans to bring Qasen in, and then those two met, and a relationship happened." *Sabtaza.* A woman who behaved erratically.

Keð bit her lower lip. The capped streetlights turned on, illuminating the crevices, cracks, and uplifts in the cobblestones around them. "I wouldn't have expected someone in Asraqan to have a single-digit parallel name."

"People move to Asraqan from 5th all of the time," Tantas said. "He's from 11th."

"Let's just drop it." It was stupid to be fighting when alert messages lurked in the Stream.

When they reached their unit, Tantas fidgeted with the door until it unlocked. It swung open. Keð shut the door behind them with her foot and adjusted the bags so she could lock it. The *click* as the double-bolt engaged calmed some of her anxiety.

They put the food away in silence. Keð didn't meet Tantas' eyes, instead focusing on what had gone wrong in that conversation. She had hidden every wince at hearing other-Keð's name. It must have been something during the nightmare, some betrayal that Keð wasn't just polished BC neutrality — that she actually cared about the superstitions. You never married someone with the same name as a sibling, not even when you left a family to form a sinåmn household.

People in Sò Hóta and Sò Găn duplicated names frequently, often separating themselves from siblings with *younger* or *older*. It had never bothered her there.

Keð kept the prepared dumplings on the table and took out the soup pot and steamer. The broth went in below. She broke apart tough leaves into the two metal baskets. In one, she set the meat-and-vegetable-filled dumplings, rectangular and open like overflowing purses; in the other, the ear-shaped dumplings filled with pureed leafy vegetables mixed with bright orange tubers, their color bleeding into the well-shaped dough. She assembled everything over the pot and turned on the burner.

Tantas finished separating the cold-storage food between the freezer and refrigerator. Keð leaned back against the counter and murmured, "What do you want me to do?"

"I don't know that there's anything at this point." Tantas sighed and folded up the bags. She arranged them neatly in the empty drawer by Keð's left hand.

Keð sighed. "Why did you go sinåmn, Tantas? When you got engaged, you said—"

"All families have to end someday," Tantas said. "It's the way that things work."

"But why *ours*? I mean, we said—"

"I'm going to call Zoðr." Tantas turned away and went towards her bag.

Keð closed her eyes, trying to breathe and clear her mind so that the tears wouldn't come.

The moodiness being about Wiren and Lilinbaðụ's festival was neater and tidier than the reality in front of her and the reason their parents knew they needed to make up. Bhamsă was right — Vait had been uncanny in his ability to find her vulnerability based on scant facts.

The data couldn't describe the emptiness in her parents' home in Asraqan. The rooms let out to boarders should have been filled with family members — their grandparents, womb-mother, and uncle's family, and two more children. *It should have been filled*, but beyond the four of them and a few distant relatives she barely knew, it was *itleren nåmċen baðụ*, an empty jar overturned.

If Tantas felt badly about what she'd said, it didn't show in the exaggerated *hello* yelled as she waved at the wall camera. Keð circled around Tantas to avoid being on screen, bound for her own tablet. She tethered in and declined interfacing with the wall camera infrastructure.

There were nine alerts.

Two travel advisories — which would have also been on Tantas' tablet, meaning Tantas had ignored them. One high-priority message from Bhamsă. Six group messages from the BC. Keð checked the travel advisories first.

Military action in the heartland. Qoziðamn was just outside of the 205-kilometer alert zone. Bhamsă's message described the situation in a series of bulleted lists, with four attachments describing everything in detail. Keð couldn't review a hundred and thirty pages that night. The most important thing was that she was on standby.

Bhamsă's message concluded, *You may be summoned to Tamiðamn, from which six people are currently marked missing. It's two towns away. Someone will meet you on the train if that happens and give you a better briefing. The commanding officer does not currently believe it is necessary.* Keð had no guns. Her stomach churned. This wasn't good.

Qoziðamn residents commuted via train or cooperative vehicle to nearby Bonðamn and, if they were a specialist shared by the district, Tamiðamn.

Some of the rebels involved in the fighting had come from Tamiðamn. The village shone bright red in the heat map — five kilometers into the alert zone, yet still under lockdown. Everything had happened overnight.

So absorbed was Keð in the officers' message chatter that she didn't look up to check the dumplings until the stock foamed up over the rim and splattered onto the burner. She threw her tablet down on the luggage and hastened to turn the burner down. The tablet clunked awkwardly onto the floor and slid onto its side.

Tantas turned from her video chat with Zoðr, brow furrowed, eyes angry. Keð winced and mouthed an apology. A ghost of broth sizzled against the outer bottom of the soup pot, leaving discoloration where it sputtered into vapor.

She finished the dumplings in the kitchen. The read receipt on the messages would show Keð was engaged. It was useless to do anything other than prepare.

CHAPTER SEVEN

NO SUMMONS CAME.

On the second evening in Qoziðamn, it stormed. Shields came down automatically to protect the rental unit's windows from hail, ice, and wind. It was as if the mountain goddess — whose name was made of clicks like pebbles, not the familiar syllables Keð had guessed at first sight — struck boulders as they fell from great heights.

It sounded enough like BC fighting that Keð couldn't sleep. Instead, she read through the main section headers of Bhamsă's attachments, focusing on what she needed to know for sleepy villages like Qoziðamn.

AI had performed an anonymized communications sentiment analysis among the seven villages in Heartland Zone 38-14. About eighteen families in total had members at risk for joining the rebels, only one in Qoziðamn. Most were already in custody. The rebellion had even made the news, spun as an illegal technology ring.

The announcers, Keð's parents, and Tantas' family didn't understand wireless broadcast technology. People in the BC did. Some young individualists had decided to make their own radio station and a wireless Stream network. The electromagnetic radiation would deteriorate in space, but not fast enough to meet the stringent *very small, albeit nonzero*, requirements for the probability of signal detection at two light-years.

The Blackout relied on ensuring that Maðz showed no signs of advanced civilization: Laser interference to make any transit-viewers see an atmosphere hostile to every form of life imaginable and tight control on the type and directionality of EM. Almost all permitted technology connected to the network via tether or the limited-access EM bands that deteriorated significantly before reaching the edge of the solar system.

It was overkill, in Keð's opinion. The existing signal had a wide area from Maðz's nearly seventeen thousand years of human activity, now donut-shaped from the twenty-five hundred year Blackout. For most of human history, no one had realized that there were beings in space that would kill other intelligent species without reason or due process. Now that this was a reality, planetary protection meant sacrifice. Keð would have loved to receive news updates between tether points. However, she respected limits even when a Blackout regulation made no technological or scientific sense. Safety relied on a sense of community and mutual recognition of what could happen if it broke.

Wiren hadn't always respected limits.

Keð set her tablet down and stared up at the ceiling. She focused on her breathing to expel the intrusive thoughts. It was not auspicious to have a dead comrade worm her way into Keð's mind.

The deluge outside stopped three hours later, and the storm windows retracted themselves.

Keð wandered back into the room and slipped into the bed beside Tantas. She fell asleep almost instantly and dreamed of the taiga in Sò Hóta.

She awoke again to a small crackling noise. Moonlight bathed the room in much the same way as it had when she'd fallen asleep. Wiren stood in front of the curtains, blood pouring down the front of her BC uniform. Blood bubbled from her mouth as she tried to speak, hands gesticulating. The room was frigid, and Tantas still lay asleep.

It wouldn't do to have a ghost in a room with a pregnant woman. Keð slipped out of the bed and put her socks on before her feet touched the tiles. Wiren stopped attempting to whisper.

"What do you want?" Keð murmured once she reached the end of the bed. "Why are you doing this? It's not time for the dead to haunt the living." The spirit-worker had also been full of it, Keð wanted to add. She should never have burned the charm.

Wiren glanced at the tablet at Keð's bedside, tethered and waiting. Keð hadn't turned on the light.

This ghost spoke in a muddled whisper like shadows of insect wings passing through leaves in summer. Keð couldn't make out words. Wiren spat sticky, black blood on the floor between them. It oozed between the cracks in the tile. She scowled.

"I can't understand a word," Keð whispered. "What are you *here*? You're dead."

Wiren turned towards the window and pointed up towards one of the mountains, whose snow-capped peaks remained illumined in the darkness, cross-long towards Bonðamn and Tamiðamn.

"Is there something out there?"

Tantas stirred in the bed. Keð turned towards her and prayed silently for her to remain asleep. Tantas' eyes opened, and her hand touched the empty space Keð had occupied only moments ago.

Wiren looked at Tantas, too. She stepped back until half of her body lay within the outer wall and window, burning the glass black where she touched it.

Keð's sister saw Wiren and screamed. She grabbed Keð's pillow and held it in front of herself like a shield.

The ghost disappeared in a flurry of ice shards that hit the floor like marbles rolling, and she disappeared into the grout between the floor tiles.

Keð jumped sideways onto the bed and grabbed Tantas. She pulled the pillow down until they were face-to-face. "It's okay. She—*it*—it's gone."

"Was that—"

"Wiren, yeah."

Tantas started crying. She brought her knees to her chest. Keð turned the light on. The windows remained black where the ghost had touched them. Even though Tantas had booked the room, Keð had a feeling that it was BC's responsibility to pay for repairs. It was a BC ghost, after all, lurking in Keð's vacation time.

The blackish-brown blood Wiren had spat still lay where it had fallen. Keð avoided touching it. "It was in your house, in the guest bedroom," Keð said. She turned towards the door.

"Don't leave me here!"

"I need some disposable napkins to clean this up. Wiren died during a conflict. There's blood."

Tantas wiped the base of her palms across her cheeks and sniffled. Her voice shook as she asked, "Did you go to a specialist? How long has this been happening?"

"He told me to burn my anti-Wiren charm on the last day of Lilinbaðu's festival."

"You should get your money back. Gods, what's the point of a spirit-worker if he can't even do basic warding against the dead?"

Keð paused with her hand on the door hook. Her brow furrowed. "The specialist asked me if Wiren was really dead. He didn't have a protocol for this. I brushed it all off as some kind of money-making thing. What if Wiren—"

"That was a ghost. Wiren is *really dead*." Tantas sniffled again. "I need—"

"I'll get you one."

Keð thumbed the latch and opened the door. The darkness of the kitchen and living area only had the specter of their dirty dishes from the night before. She found the compostable towels in the utility shelving beneath the sink and brought the entire roll into the bedroom.

Tantas took one and blew her nose. Keð cleaned up the ghost goo and threw it in with the incinerable trash. That way, the ghost's remains wouldn't contaminate Heartland compost.

"Why would Wiren be haunting you? What did you do?" Tantas' eyes narrowed accusingly.

Keð sighed. "Bhamsă, our Dispatcher, originally had me slated to accompany her on the mission where she died. I was moved off of that at the last minute, something procedural. They needed someone with a working knowledge of remote mountain culture in Sò Hóta to gather intelligence related to some sentiment analysis we'd done. People were unhappy."

"What's sentiment analysis?"

"We do aggregated looks at what people say on the Stream and try to predict unrest before it happens to prevent things like the situation farther into the Heartland," Keð said. "The Heartland people probably communicated using flat paper, not smart paper or tablets. Sentiment analysis is AI, and it maintains user privacy. Don't worry about it — nobody's going to read your romantic letters to Zoðr."

Tantas glanced at her tablet. "But you could, right?"

"Theoretically, with a warrant. The AI takes care of flagging people."

"But what if the AI is wrong and you're just looking at someone's life? Like everything in it, all of the fights with spouses and kids and—"

"The technology is over a thousand years old. It works just fine." It didn't always, but a post-ghost-sighting argument with a shaken sibling was not in Keð's playbook for smoothing things over.

"Did you read Zo—"

"I looked at Zoðr's public Stream profile," Keð said. "The BC officer privileges aren't that different from what you have in the regular police station. We have the audit control module and access to things like health records and purchase history without warrants."

Tantas shook her head. "Some things are private."

"Some things are issues of international security."

"So, Dispatcher Bhamsă switched you to a different project," Tantas said. "Anything else?"

Keð said no quickly. Wiren hadn't known about her and Bhamsă — the relationship hadn't even started until two months before Wiren's death. Dead Wiren might — the dead knew so much.

Wiren hadn't pointed at Keð when asked why it was here. It had pointed at the mountains, towards the international military presence.

Keð needed to read up on the villages, starting with Tamiðamn.

"Have you thought about offering a sacrifice to see what Wiren wants? So the ghost can talk to you?"

A ghost needed blood to speak. Blood sacrifice to the dead required animals with red coats, usually karål or tekåċ, the latter more budget-friendly and frequently stocked at the properties of established ritualists for the dead. Lilinbaðụ had hundreds of red-coated tekåċ in her possession, enough for the handful of true hauntings that happened each year.

Here in the mountains, Keð didn't know where to begin at finding a competent ritualist, acquiring a karål or tekåċ, and even storing a live animal until Wiren appeared again. She almost said so, but it would have looked standoffish.

"A bit, yeah. We should go back to bed."

"I don't know if I can sleep."

Keð yawned. "Wiren isn't haunting *you*. She didn't die at your house."

Tantas sighed. "Not the point, but whatever."

Keð returned to her side of the bed and pulled off her socks. Tantas turned off the light as Keð got back under the thick duvet and blankets.

As her eyes adjusted, the contours of the mountain reappeared, sky only partially cloudy. Snowflakes gusted in front of the window. No Wiren. Tantas tossed and turned beside her, but eventually stilled into sleep.

It was Keð who remained awake until dawn peeled back the night, who fell asleep to fitful dreams of wandering in the mountain forests. The mountain goddess walked ahead of her, beckoning into the darkness. The shades of landslide and exposure victims seethed in the darkness. Keð followed her until she heard her womb-mother's voice screaming her own name. The mountain goddess stopped walking. She turned towards Keð and stared at her with eyes the color that Keð imagined an abyss would have, like staring down from a great height without knowing what lay at the bottom.

CHAPTER EIGHT

THE SNOW AND ice melted during the morning, filling the air with a muddy, clean smell. Tantas and Keð checked out muck boots out at the main house and went for a walk. The sticky ground sucked at Keð's boots, leaving heavy-cleat prints behind her.

The smell of karål and earthy manure grew stronger the closer they came to the fenced-in pasture where the karål were kept to fertilize the ground before spring planting. One karål met Keð's eyes and snorted, six nostrils flaring in its flat face. Its mate bleated.

Tantas went right up to the fence and set her elbows down on it, cupping her chin. "It's so nice up here. It's like our old home. The ċiza grazing there."

Keð let out a tense puff of air and stopped at the fence beside her. The mountains reminded her of the hills at 5th parallel, certainly, but this was inland, not the coastal peninsula in the village before Asraqan.

The mudslide had ended their home village, Sabtuzo, when Keð was four and Tantas was two. It was Ruin A347 now.

"I had a dream about Mom last night," Keð said.

"Me, too." Tantas took a sharp breath in. She moved her hands to grip the fence as if the light breeze would carry her through the air if she let go. "Do you mind if I tell you something?"

"Go on."

"Wiren isn't the first ghost I've seen. It's — I wasn't going to tell you. We'd said we wouldn't tell you."

Keð looked hard at her sister.

"Zoðr and I went on a camping trip the summer before we married — down to the park by Sabtuzo," Tantas said. "We pitched a tent and went hiking one evening during the full moon. There were ghosts in the ruins milling like wisps of smoke in the silvery light. One of them saw us and followed us back to camp. We had to find someone to perform an exorcism."

The karål closest to them bleated and approached the fence. Keð held out her hand. It sucked her fingers into its muscular mouth, massaging her hand gently with its wide, flat mastication teeth that lay in rings. Its cover-chomping teeth, sharp like scythes, remained retracted.

Keð drew away from the karål gently after about a minute. She said, "You went back."

"I didn't want you to worry," Tantas murmured. "Anyway, the one who told us about the ritualist actually *lived* in the ruins, an older ximsa-gender person named Men Toðo. Le'd known our family growing up, especially our womb-mother. They were really close during and after her pregnancies. Le had a house cobbled together and dug out from what the landslide left, you know, after the state authorities came through and salvaged tech and metal and bodies. No Stream connection, no running water, just sturdy walls. I can't imagine what it must be like to live for decades among the haunting dead. The one who followed me and Zoðr was a young girl, maybe eight or nine. She kept crying outside of the tent. It was one of the worst sounds I have ever heard."

Living off-Stream sounded exactly like a ximsa in mourning. Keð reached out and started stroking the karål's head. "And the ghost never came in through the tent?"

"No." Tantas squeezed her eyes shut and breathed in raggedly. "She'd died of suffocation in one of the houses, I think. The ghost-body was horrific."

"How did the ximsa live there without being possessed or consumed by ghosts?"

Tantas shrugged. "The ximsa wore a charm from a ritualist down there, and that ritualist had also warded the outside of that patchwork house with phrases from the *Book of Lost Souls*. We sought lim out. It was expensive, maybe 200 credits, for the exorcism."

"Why are you telling me this?" Keð imagined what kind of message Bhamsă would send after reviewing Keð's expense accounts and seeing an exorcism. It was bad enough to have the charm listed there.

Tantas sighed. "We didn't intend to do a sinåmn house. During the ritual, we had a message from our grandparents. One of the old pictograms for severance. It was in mud at the edge of the ritual circle. I can't imagine a ghost who would willingly approach a salt barrier like that. The ritualist interpreted it that way — that we had to go sinåmn. And we decided not to tell you or our parents that —"

"It could have just been lim playing with you."

"I know. We went to an oracle and had it read for us. It said the same thing, basically. 'Trees cut down in the forest make way for new growth.'" Tantas sighed and reached out to pet the karål. It snapped at her fingers, and Tantas drew her hand back with a yelp.

Keð stopped stroking it.

"We'd already planned a family welcoming ritual and had to redo everything. We really didn't intend a sinåmn. And I knew you'd be mad." Tantas squeezed her eyes shut. "Whatever happened between you and Wiren, you need to fix it."

"I know."

"Are you involved in anything that would make it angry? Did you fail at something?"

Keð shook her head.

"Are you sure you don't—"

"My dispatcher and I had sex," Keð said softly. "That's a failure. It's not what Wiren would be after. I don't think Bhamsă took me off of that mission for any personal reasons. Le's not like that."

"Is a relationship like that allowed?"

"No."

"Keð Teðqawo!" Tantas' shout caught her off-guard. A few oğam working among the herd turned to stare at the two women.

Keð shrugged. "It's complicated. Love stuff."

"Isn't le an acim? You're going to get old and die, and le's just going to go on." Tantas' face scrunched up in disgust. "What's the age difference? Five hundred? A *thousand*?"

"Not, um, as bad as it could be." Keð's face felt hot. "Can we just stop talking about that? I'm only mentioning it to point out—"

"Are you serious?" Tantas shook her head. "If I were a dead person who learned about this, I'd sure haunt you until you changed your mind and broke up with lim. That's just crazy."

Keð sucked her tongue against her teeth. "It isn't here to give me spectral dating advice."

"How do you know?"

"It was pointing at the mountain." Keð nodded at the near-distant peak. A train snaked across a mountain bridge.

Tantas turned her head and scrutinized the mountain. "I find that less than believable."

"That's what it was doing when you woke up screaming." Keð stuck out her tongue, ineffective because Tantas wasn't even looking. The karål was, and it snorted. "I'm on standby. It's probably something to do with that."

"Does Wiren's death have anything to do with the mountains?"

"No."

"Do you understand why it sounds like you're reaching?" Tantas sighed.

Keð worked her boots into the mud until the ground cover's roots twisted up towards the sky, pallid as worms. A damp breeze tugged at the nape of her neck. Tantas leaned her hand forward towards the karål and gave it a few clumsy strokes on the top of its head.

"You didn't tell me that you were on standby," Tantas murmured. "I thought—"

Keð shook her head. "It's nothing to worry about. They've probably added retirees to the standby, too. BC just wants people on hand if the situation gets out of control."

"And if you're fucking your commanding officer, le probably won't pick you first if things go bad," Tantas said matter-of-factly. She pursed her lips together and smiled, then elbowed Keð in the side. "I'm sorry. *Fuck*, lighten up."

It wasn't a joke to make aloud, but Tantas couldn't hurt her with it. It only mattered if other BC officers heard. Keð breathed in and out until the pit in her stomach relaxed. Tantas only possessed Yellow clearance and would probably never interact professionally with anyone above Green, those in official government positions, or the stray national officers who had barely failed the final exams to make BC.

Anything above Green required sacrifice. BC officers had Indigo clearance. The demimortals occupied Indigo and Violet clearance, and they'd been absorbed against their will into collective consciousnesses. Theoretically, immortals called *iqamnim* had the highest level of clearance, Black, but Maðz had no iqamnim. Other worlds did.

"A peace offering," Keð said softly. She held out her hand. "You don't talk about Bhamsă, and I won't stare at you like that when you talk about why you went sinåmn."

Tantas took it and squeezed. "Deal."

They walked to the trailhead beyond the pasture. Keð stopped to examine the mountain peaks again. According to the dream, something was there. According to Wiren, it was important.

Keð was on standby. It shouldn't have been her problem.

CHAPTER NINE

TAMIÐAMN, THE VILLAGE in the red zone, had fewer households than Qoziðamn — thirty-nine. Six missing people, most likely rebels. Soldiers moving through to secure the area had interviewed the village's mayor, a man named Zontas, with an AI analysis follow-up.

The data looked good enough for Keð to follow it on her tablet without feeling claustrophobic from the small screen. At an Authority Station — the term BC used for its one- to two-room BC station in every village — Keð could have used larger monitors and better equipment to navigate the analyses, but she'd need approval from Bhamsǎ first.

The red dot to the left of the data file's name meant that no one had verified the AI's work. The assignment annotations from active officers indicated a very hot situation in the mountains, with the rebels holding strong — armed with a mixture of stolen livestock prods, tasers, and 3D-printed or hand-forged ammunition. Busy officers wouldn't care about follow-up in a remote village.

Among Tamiðamn's missing six were two men, aged 21 and 34, who had done continuing education in terraced farming techniques through the VR extension school, hardware programming on the side. A ximsa, aged 22, had dropped out of the police academy in Asraqan. Among the two atan, aged 28 and 31, one kept ler chain-lineage family's household running and had questionable movie tastes. The other had floated among a menagerie of extension school courses in everything from philosophy to electrical maintenance. All had the background to make illegal devices.

A message popped up. She navigated to her inbox. It was Vait — a photograph of a beach with a surfboard. Keð sent back one of her photographs from the hiking trail, which looked out towards the mountains.

You're geolocated to Qoziðamn, he responded. *Does this mean you're on standby?*

Keð rolled her eyes. She started to type *Yes*, but instead said, *You could always look at my file with your privileges. Why aren't you?*

Vait said nothing. Keð toggled back to the review screen and skimmed through the work she'd already done to reacquaint herself. She read the last rebel profile twice.

Tað Wir, family name Bawimot, aged 22, did not match the AI profile for a radical. Transcripts from the initial officer interview with Mayor Zontas hadn't recorded Tað Wir's name, either.

She was a young woman with black umber skin like Keð's. The surname *Bawimot* usually meant that someone had moved inland from the coast. Keð's stomach flip-flopped at the hair, though — blood-red, no evidence in the roots of dyeing. Tamiðamn had no specialists in it, either. Tað hadn't checked out a bicycle or taken a train in the past few weeks. The roots would have shown if she'd had it done in a town. The purchase history module had no record of paying for hair color services.

Another message came in. Keð went into focus mode to silence it.

Tað had no background in technology. She'd matriculated into the extension school for advanced studies in wildlife management, a strange career choice for a woman. Mamltaqal's strict gender roles meant that in the mountains, almost all wildlife managers would be oğam or ximsa. Tað had no flags or warnings about her on the Stream; no one had ever blocked her on VR or chat modules for poor behavior.

The University of Asraqan listed Tað's application for advanced studies as *pending* in the system. The examination results had yet to come in, but based on Tað's performance in extension school courses, Keð knew it would be far above average. The family information was equally unremarkable: Her home was chain-lineage, eighth generation, grandparents and both great-grandparents still alive and in the house. Keð clicked through. Everyone had come from Ðolųzam, a village not far from Ruin A347. They'd relocated just after the disaster that had killed Keð's family. Keð's stomach tightened. It was such a strange coincidence.

The woman's record would remain flagged until Keð eliminated her from the pool. Keð upgraded the other five to *likely involved* and saved the changes to the database. Tað was different.

She navigated back to her messages. Vait had said, *You know you can request comp time, right?* A form was attached.

Keð looked up at Tantas. She wrote back, *Do you really think that I should ask to go in?*

Vait said, *I wouldn't, but you're you.*

Thanks, I think.

She set down the tablet and looked up at the ceiling. Vait didn't know what she'd found. If she volunteered to go in, Bhamsǎ might send her into combat. She picked up the tablet. *An uncanny coincidence,* she wrote, *being here at just the right time.*

Only the Gods can see the whole of time, Vait wrote. *Don't think about it too much. It'll fuck up your head.*

You're not sober, she wrote.

Correct.

When she picked up the tablet, she looked at the Stream chatter among the officers. Five had conducted roll calls, all in peripheral villages like Tamiðamn. The three at the center of the AKTI's modeled radio signal report had little data and few team-wide updates — all bad news. Two central villages had almost completely revolted. Quelling them would take more than a slap on the wrist. Eighty-three Sentinel robots had been activated. Civilians were dying. Keð would be activated sooner or later if she didn't control her own fate.

Tantas came out of the bedroom and joined Keð on the couch, clutching a cup of qụmsa close.

She only needed four days maximum. Keð composed a message to Bhamsă — *hey, I'm reviewing documents, can we talk?* — and made eye contact with Tantas. It was too early to say anything yet.

A message appeared from Bhamsă: *Are you working from vacation? What is going on?*

Keð said, "I need to call my Dispatcher."

"Could this wait until after dinner?"

"Depends on Bhamsă. What are we eating?"

Tantas pushed herself off of the couch and walked into the kitchen area. She opened the refrigerator and pulled out ụkrsn. "Could you put together dough?"

Keð typed a fast message to Bhamsă: *I think one of the people in Tamiðamn isn't with the rebels. Look at Tað Wir Bawimot. It could be a hostage case or a missing person.* She set the tablet down and followed Tantas into the kitchen. "Do we want filled flatbread?"

"That will work." Tantas pulled out a cutting board. "Zoðr says the news looks bad up here. We might go back early. I might."

"That isn't necessary. The fighting is several hundred kilometers away, barely in this district," Keð offered. She took out the flour box and weighed 500 grams in a mixing bowl. "People have family, definitely, but I'm not in uniform, so nobody would know."

Tantas nodded. "You don't have weapons?"

"No. I could do a Sentinel connection in Qoziðamn Central, but Bhamsă hasn't asked that of me yet. I could put in a request for a weapons delivery." Keð brought the measuring cup over to the sink and filled it with comfortably warm water. She worked it into the dough slowly. The br grain started to come together in sienna-colored clumps.

"What does a Sentinel look like?"

Tantas had been too young to remember everything that had happened when they were buried in the library in the center of town, their parents huddled over them praying. The library's wide open spaces and sturdy construction had made it good for surviving.

Rescue Sentinels looked nominally human to facilitate interacting with scared people trapped in dangerous situations. They had stun technology, nothing lethal.

Sentinels in villages, towns, and cities comprised the Distributed Warfare Network, controllable only by BC officers, demimortals, and the theoretical iqamnim. They did not look human.

Keð worked her hands into the dough. "Imagine something with guns installed in its arms, with a two-second refill rate from a chamber in its chest, microprocessors, and then add more guns. Usually, there's one for every two hundred people in remote areas. Very small villages have generalist Sentinels. Villages like Qoziðamn will have four, each of them built differently — one for speed, one for jumping, climbing, and rough terrain, a generalist, and something for brute force."

"How many people can they kill per minute?"

"A lot of people." The dough was now a supple ball. Keð used the back of her hand to get into the cabinet and pulled out one of the other cutting boards. She sprinkled more flour down.

Tantas cut into the meat. "Do they take hostages?"

"Sentinels aren't programmed for that. People don't like killing other people. Sentinels supplement us. Once they're activated, they make decisions based on programming, and they protect officers. You can't — when they decide who needs to die, unless given orders to reserve someone for questioning, they shoot to kill." Keð squatted down and peered into the cabinet for a rolling pin. She delicately worked it out from among the other cooking utensils, leaving powdery br flour in her hands' wake. "That's why we rely so much on AI sentiment analysis and try to de-escalate first. Nobody wants a bloodbath in a report."

"How many people have you been instrumental in killing?"

"Two, personally. Nobody by Sentinel. One was a suicide after I took him into custody. The other tried to kill me."

"You're not responsible for a suicide." Tantas put down the knife.

"We count those in the statistics because they shouldn't happen. My record is good — I have 95% fewer kills than most officers in my cohort." Keð dusted the rolling pin. "Are you trying to figure out what I'll have to do if they call me in?"

"Yeah."

Keð opened the container of dried herbs and sprinkled it over the half-rolled flatbread. "I reviewed reports. There's a missing woman about your age, last Stream check-in a few hours before the military exchanged fire with the rebels in retreat."

"Not a rebel?"

"If you wanted to kill someone, this is a good time to do it. Everyone marked missing is a suspect. Kill her, throw the body in the woods — maybe high up in the mountains, if you're smart about it — and everyone will think she was fatally injured in one of the firefights." The green and red spices bled into the dough as Keð rolled it out. It bounced back elastically each time it touched the edge of the cutting board, sending flour onto the counter in thin lines. "I checked Tamiðamn because it's close, and if I'm sent anywhere, I want it to be there. And I'm troubled. The woman's face hasn't been identified in the data check-ins from the engagement zone."

"So you want to find her." Tantas breathed out sharply. "In a travel advisory zone where anyone could decide to shoot you."

"That's the plan, yeah. Wiren was pointing at the mountains. Maybe it's this."

Tantas washed her hands and dried them on a towel. "Ghosts don't care about other people. They're jealous of the living and protective of the lives they once had. Wiren and this *whoever* have nothing to do with each other."

"That was real blood on the floor. Normal ghosts don't leave real blood." Keð stopped rolling out the dough. "Could you hand me the tray from the mini-oven?"

"It's a haunting deception."

"No. I put it in with the trash. It soaked into the disposable towel like old blood," Keð said. Her gut clenched into a knot. "It left real mud on the duvet back at your house. The ritualist I saw told me that this wasn't a haunting, that Wiren didn't seem dead. That's what puzzled him."

Tantas greased the tray and set it down in front of the cutting board. She worked the oil that lingered on her fingertips into the back of her hands and wrists. Keð transferred the br flatbread into the pan and turned on the tap with her elbow to wash her hands.

"What would it be other than a ghost?"

"Something to do with the mountain." Keð turned off the tap and reached for a towel.

Tantas sighed. "Take your vid in the bedroom, I guess. I'm not going to argue with you. I think it's insane, but if you're after a missing person, it's somewhat dutiful."

"I'll only be gone for a few days." Keð put the bread in the oven and set the timer. "We're here until we finish out the decad, right?"

"Yeah."

Keð had fifteen minutes. She walked back to her tablet and checked her messages before she untethered. *Are you willing to sacrifice vacation time for this?*

In the bedroom, she tethered in. Outside, the sky held puffy white clouds. The dark bodies of karål were mere specks on the distant terraces, stretching as far as Keð could see in a patchwork of forests colored chlorophyll green and retinal purple.

Keð entered the queue for Bhamsă and leaned her head against the wall. She adjusted herself on the pillows.

Bhamsă took the call after five minutes. Bhamsă always wore well-hemmed plainclothes, sophisticated and solid-colored, today a patchwork of amber, orange, and yellow.

A classy, gold-tipped glass bubbled with shimmering amber alcohol. Bhamsă took a sip while Keð greeted lim with Mamltab pleasantries, the high-register speech falling awkwardly. "Some say that the road may bring a good person like that one." *Ćera manezoz ćowe nwųm sanqųð akemesr be tatbek.*

"I think that we can avoid pronoun substitution," Bhamsă said curtly. "How are you?"

"Fine."

"How's your sister?"

Keð cleared her throat. "I told her I might go to Tamiðamn. She's not happy — she's thinking of leaving early." In Sò Gǎms, she said, "We're rocky with each other because I cannot attend the birthing ceremony for her child."

Bhamsă sighed and said in Sò Gǎms, "I'm sure she can hear that you switched to a different language. House walls aren't thick." Le switched back to Mamltab. "Do you really want to do this search? Keðtimi, we can't spare someone to bring you equipment right now. The Authority Station in Qoziðamn will have some things, at the very least a taser or maybe an old handgun. They might not even work. Tamiðamn has two Sentinels and some outdated equipment. That's what has hurt us so far — we never anticipated rebels here. Someone had to do an aircraft drop. If you wanted to volunteer, we would rather send you to the war zone."

The *-timi* diminutive made Keð blush. She almost didn't process what Bhamsă said about the aircraft. They required significant paperwork to use, as each flight needed wireless navigation and communication signaling. It was not Blackout-friendly technology. "Are you serious?"

"The rebels have some kind of scrambler that disables Sentinels," Bhamsă said. "We'll have to kill all of them and confiscate the equipment to fix the vulnerabilities. It's messy."

Keð looked up at the bare gray ceiling and closed her eyes. "May I register with the Sentinels in Tamiðamn?"

"That's fine." Bhamsă frowned. "Anything else?"

"I want comp time — five days for my sister's birthing ceremony."

Bhamsă sipped ler alcohol. "I see."

Keð asked, "How much do you know about the role of women and atan siblings in naming rituals?"

Bhamsă's eyes glazed over, a sign that le didn't know, that le'd fallen back on the expertise of people within the acimta's hive-collective who had grown up in Mamltaqal. That annoyed Keð the most about Bhamsă, how it was a reflex even when Keð wanted to say something personal. "It's important."

"Tantas wants me there."

"It's a long way from your post." Bhamsă gritted ler teeth.

"I know." The corners of Keð's lips flinched towards a smile. Her heart sank. "I am reporting for duty to find this girl, Tað Wir Bawimot. I don't need time with my sister — just the ride down, the two-day ritual, the ride back up. Not much. I think this is worth my time."

Bhamsă shook ler head. "Keðtimi, we will have to see." Le paused. "If I say yes — and that is *if* — you could be called to the fighting zones at any time. You understand that?"

"I understand."

"And as far as your comp time goes, we will have to see. It would look like favoritism if I just gave it to you."

"Vait sent me paperwork. You have to do something if I file it."

"*Approve* or *disapprove*," Bhamsă said. "Just because you file something doesn't mean I will say *yes*. I'm transferring two protocol documents to you regarding missing persons, along with some intelligence information about the current engagement. Please read it and stay out of everyone's way. Have you checked the audit modules for Tað Wir Bawimot?"

"No," Keð said.

"I just did. They're interesting."

"Anything else?"

"No, that's it." Bhamsă smiled and shook ler head. "I miss you, Keð. We'll have a good time catching up when we're both back home. Be safe."

Home, Bhamsă had called it. Keð forced herself to a smile. She wasn't sure she could ever call Dukkă home, no matter how much time she spent there. "Yeah," she said. "I miss you, too."

Something banged in the kitchen. Keð turned her head towards the door. "Goodbye," she said.

"Goodbye."

Out in the kitchen, a starburst of glass lay across the floor. It came from something the color of the rental's drinking cups. Tantas stood on the other side of the high table separating the kitchen from the remainder of the room.

The twisted glass had a pattern completely unlike any starburst. It had no sharp edges from being dropped.

It spelled a name in alphatonal characters from Dukkă, a message that Tantas could never hope to read.

The Village of Strong Branches, it read in Sò Gǎms. In Mamltab, it would make *Taŏ Cewirim Nabu Oċezo*.

Taŏ Wir. *Strong Branch*. Keð's brow furrowed. Wiren, *branched*. Two names, both containing the word *wir*. If Keð had held any doubt about Wiren's intentions, it disappeared in the glittering message written in a language common to them.

Ghosts did not break household cups apart into twisted glass to confirm they wanted someone to travel towards a village where a young woman had gone missing. Keð knelt just in front of the broken shards and worked her fingertips across the writing. The edges felt smooth beneath her fingertips.

The dried mud. Blood. Now this. She met Tantas' wide eyes.

It was something darker, perhaps miraculous, that had drawn Wiren out of death. Whatever it was lay in Tamiðamn, the village where Taŏ Wir lived.

CHAPTER TEN

KEÐ PACKED ENOUGH clothes for two days and stopped by the Qoziðamn Authority Station to find weapons. The two-room unit had seen better days. Mold bloomed along two of the walls, and the thermostat regulator didn't respond to her touch.

She had a choice between a taser that barely worked and a gun that hadn't been serviced in years. She tethered in to check out the gun, and she put in a work order for someone to service the Authority Station.

In the gun's case lay an old, portable wood icon to the mountain goddess. It was cracked and warped from many humid summers, but its features remained distinct: Large breasts, vine-like hair that had once been painted green, and skin as black as the fertile mountain soil beneath the slumbering volcanoes. It felt numinous in Keð's hands, so she did an oblation before it and set it in her overnight bag.

The morning work train was just pulling away when Keð arrived at the station, and the next one wouldn't come for another hour. She considered going back to Tantas.

Instead, she went to the store, almost empty at this hour, and bought a sleeping bag. If Tamiðamn's Authority Station bore any resemblance to Qoziðamn's, she'd rather take the questions from Bhamsă.

The train stopped eight times before Tamiðamn, six of them train links to more remote agricultural working areas. Keð arrived in the middle of the day and only caught a bare glimpse of the small labyrinth of houses that fanned out from Tamiðamn's two impressive buildings, the Tamiðamn Central office building and the library.

She didn't notice the acenbomon until after she detrained and stopped on the platform. The apotropaic tree trunk loomed over her, crisscrossed with swaths of brightly-colored fabric and painted with horrific, bright eyes.

A few others started when they saw it, but kept walking. Keð couldn't. She'd only seen an acenbomon once before — during news coverage of a disease outbreak in Taðaqan when eleven hundred people died. There, the hundred eyes had warded the city from evil in all directions, accompanied by the comforting voice of an announcer who guided viewers through the old folk practice's rationale.

No village put up an acenbomon unless something horrible had happened. Keð had never heard of one used after BC and national soldiers moved into an area.

The train's lurch away from the platform drew Keð out of her thoughts. She took the steps down from the platform and circled the trunk. Every painted eye faced the forest. An impromptu stone altar at its base held the remains of burnt offerings, barely cool.

Keð bowed her head solemnly and ignored the cakey, dry feeling in her mouth.

The main temple faced the train station, an ornate facility dedicated to the mountain goddess. A smaller pan-deity shrine lay beside it, a plaque in front marking it as a worship site for numerous

Mamlt gods. Tamiðamn's library and Tamiðamn Central flanked them on either side.

Behind the train station, a cluster of adults sat outside of an eatery smoking a bright indigo herb that Keð couldn't identify. The restaurant's interior looked smaller than the bedroom Keð had shared with Tantas for the past half-week.

Children played in the streets. Teenagers and adults walked into and out of the library, most of the former likely extension students, to use the communal VR facilities. Three oğam biked uphill along a path, livestock prods bouncing at their sides. With all of the routine activity, it was eerie to think that Tamiðamn lay within the BC control zone, that rebels had come from here, or that the military had done its sweep only days before. The village had been in lockdown.

BC had taught Keð not to gawk. She turned her back on the acenbomon and walked straight to Tamiðamn Central and around to the back stairs. They led up to a cramped, two-room Authority Station. The stairs down went to a holding cell for criminals.

This Authority Station had its own bathroom, unlike Qoziðamn's, but the Sentinel rack didn't fit in the operations room. Whoever had outfitted the place had set the Sentinels across from the bed such that anyone sleeping on the sagging mattress would see them first thing upon waking.

Keð interfaced with the Sentinels and winced when the two mild electric pulses verified the pairing with her implants.

Both rooms needed a heavy cleaning. Keð found two maintenance robots in a cabinet. One booted up quickly and immediately started scaling the walls and ceiling to eat the cobwebs and grime. The other wouldn't start at all. Keð spent fifteen minutes trying to find the manual to fix it. After she opened up the case and jiggled the wiring, it started normally. Keð had it vacuum the dust on the bare mattress first. There was another robot she could use, but it didn't look utility. She decided to check it later.

The Authority Station's old bedding smelled like earth and dead things. Keð set out her new star-patterned sleeping bag, which could easily fit two people. It looked out of place in the austere room.

The window looked out on the farming terraces, not the acenbomon and the village. Tamiðamn overlooked an extinct caldera lake as still as polished turquoise tiles. Smoke billowed from an active caldera in the distance.

The local equipment, despite being outdated, seemed functional. Keð picked out a baton that could open on queue into a bladed staff. She kept her gun all the same. Keð doubted she would even need Sentinels for a missing persons case.

Her tablet could interface with the fiber connection in the wall, but the Authority Station's computer didn't have the correct ports for the tablet to connect directly. She sorted through an entire drawer of dongles before concluding that she'd have to do data transfers via portable drive or secure file transfer. Keð would rather just work without the tablet.

Beneath the mass of dongles lay a briefing manual with information on the Amntaltab language, stapled together and printed in a clunky, out-of-fashion font.

She booted up the desktop computer. It was glitchy and slow, in desperate need of service. Finally, it showed her a login screen, and she typed in her credentials. When she pinged the village's mayor, Zontas, the vid didn't engage, not even to put Keð in a queue. She quit the program and went into the computer's settings to reset the hardware. The camera flickered to life, and the queue engaged.

Keð adjusted her hair and tried to look as professional as possible in plainclothes. She cleared her throat and made faces in the preview camera until she found some way to look authoritative and not so young and out of her element. The video was grainy, but it would have to do. She hit the *record* button. "Mayor Zontas, this is Keð Teðqawo Qamalin from Bilinro Cetonbasionwim. I've been assigned to your area to investigate a missing person and confirm that she's not part of the rebel engagement. Please, O Mayor, grant me information about the best time and place to meet this afternoon. Thank you, and goodbye."

She stopped the recording. Thankfully, BC officers rarely needed to use formal register in Mamltab, just formal pronouns. Zontas would use high register, depending on how much the military presence scared him.

While Keð waited for a response, she opened the Amntaltab language manual. It included mouth diagrams of how to pronounce the extra click consonants. It was dated Year 7 of the 889th Octad. It was now Year 4 of the 904th, well past that document's centennial. Asraqan's standard Mamltab changed as slowly as glass windowpanes flowed, but most mountain dialects and languages were hardly ever printed. They changed like weather. Keð threw it into the drawer.

Everyone learned Mamltab in school, anyway. Tamiðamn had kilometers of terraced farmland and a cushy, high-priority fiber connection to the lower-elevation cities in Mamltaqal. The village Streamed up petabytes of entertainment programming from the lowland cities every year. She would manage.

Zontas' reply set off a chirp. Keð walked back and sat down, ready to answer a call. It wasn't vid, but text. *I have a few minutes after I leave my grand-wixa at the library. Be there in 10 minutes.*

No formality at all. Keð frowned.

It took Keð five minutes to get everything together and leave Tamiðamn Central. The Tamiðamn Library let in so much light that she decided it had to be someone's architectural dissertation. Grilles went up and down its thick glass walls, each patterned with metallic ivy that separated painted glass scenes from national and local Mamlt myths. The mullions between each windowpane had their own specks of colored glass in auspicious shapes. The design saved on aux lighting and kept the heat in a lot better than old-fashioned glass buildings on the coast.

Keð passed the circulation consoles and entered the enormous reading room, which had windows all along the back that looked out over the terraces. That's where she wanted to be, with a view deeper into the mountains. She tapped her tongue against the back of her upper teeth as she counted the number of people: Thirty-two, none in large groups, and no sign of the mayor.

The windows lay on the other side of a set of stairs that receded into the lower floor, which hid the book stacks and VR Stream portals. She walked right up to the clear-paneled glass and linked her hands behind her back.

Twenty minutes later, the mayor came up from downstairs, flanked by a clique of locals. He had aged quickly since his last ID photo, hair white instead of gray. His skin looked like it had been lain and stretched over his bones, and he had deep laugh lines.

"Good afternoon, I am Officer Keð from the BC. You responded to my message on the Stream." She pasted a smile on her face as her Dispatcher had taught her. "Could we talk in private?"

Zontas paused a meter away from her and slow-blinked three times. Most of the clique left without Keð needing to give any direct orders. A few wandered over to the soft seating, jacked into the data streams, and put on headphones.

"This is a public place," Zontas said.

"It would have been easier in your office."

"Most have an open way of doing things here," Zontas said. He tilted his head towards a woman reading from a tethered tablet five soft seating bays away. "Tamiðamn gives you grain, you give us data, and all have an easy peace. How long have you been active in BC, officer? You're practically a girl still."

Keð decided to lie. "Ten years." Zontas couldn't check the years of service in Keð's personnel files because it required high clearance. Almost everyone took anti-aging pills to extend theirs, anyway, because the BC liked maintaining its investments. "Mamltaqal's BC unit sent soldiers through several days ago to do a sweep for forbidden technology and lawbreakers. Could you explain the acenbomon?"

"The soldiers found nothing, and the guilty people fled," Zontas said. "I don't understand why you're here. You should be in the mountains subduing rebels."

Keð folded her arms across her chest, mirroring Zontas' body language as much as possible. "I told you."

Zontas scowled. "That is just unnecessary. The village doesn't even have five hundred people in it. We know where everyone is."

"Tað Wir Bawimot?"

Zontas pursed his lips together. His nostrils flared.

Keð let silence fill the room, a soothing soundscape of people turning pages, pressing their fingers against tablet screens, and whispering in click-rich Amntaltab. She murmured, "You are their mayor. I think you know how serious it is to have someone go missing in a time like this. Why have you put up an acenbomon?"

Zontas said, "It is traditional in times of trouble. Officer, we know how this looks. The soldiers and transgressors had a firefight towards the forest. It nearly hit bystanders."

Nearly, Keð thought. Had something hit Tað Wir, the military would have noted it on Tað Wir's stream profile. "Right. So, you know that I will investigate."

The mayor let out an exasperated sigh. "How many officers are harassing peaceful villages in this area?"

Keð should have said *classified*. Instead, she told the truth. "We have thirty-four BC officers keeping the Blackout across nine villages."

"In the heavy fighting zones, far from here. I've been briefed, girl-officer." Zontas glanced beyond Keð at the terraces. "You won't find Tað Wir. She disappeared before all of this started. It's noise in the data."

Without having it in front of her, Keð couldn't remember when Tað had last logged in. She had a feeling a login had happened the same night. "Thank you for your confidence, Mayor Zontas."

"Do you need to waste my time with anything else?"

"No, that will be all. Thank you."

As Zontas turned away, Keð fought the urge to hit him in the back of the head. Instead, she clenched and relaxed her fists, watching Zontas out of her peripheral vision.

Zontas kept looking back at her like a wild animal checking to make sure a hunter hadn't seen it. Zontas knew something and was deliberately interfering with her work.

The coterie reassembled within minutes. They spoke softly in Amntaltab loudly enough that Keð could anchor her attention in the pronouns and verb endings, which were similar enough to Mamltab to catch at least vaguely. Without knowing Amntaltab, all else remained hidden.

CHAPTER ELEVEN

KEÐ REVIEWED THE drone photographs after returning to the Authority Station. She stared at the first image and traced the scenery over and over again, losing track of her thoughts each time her racing mind brought her back to Zontas in the library.

It wasn't normal behavior for a mayor, but neither was a ghost telling a person to go after a missing girl a continent away from where it had died.

She checked the sentiment analysis instead, the data color-coded and broken into twelve emotional patterns — all indexed in the appendices Keð had memorized by age thirteen. Tamiðamn had similar anxiety patterns to the other villages, peaking on the day of the military sweep. It bore no anger towards anyone, unlike the resister villages deeper in the heartland. Those graphs showed a steady, murderous orange.

Something had happened, though, on the night of Wiren's second manifestation. In the evening, the sentiment data gleaned from Tamiðamn's residents had paled from steady, cooperative purple to a bruised green. The graph swelled with red in the small hours of night like an angry, infected sore.

The acenbomon looked about a day old, judging from the hole in the ground. Zontas would have seen this data in a civilian-appropriate dashboard view, annotated by a governance AI that provided peer-reviewed analysis on what the sentiment curves meant and what he could do. Keð switched to the live data view. The fear had gotten worse since Keð's arrival.

Keð toggled back to the drone photography, took a deep breath, and willed herself to focus. The pathway taken by the soldiers in pursuit of the radicals had color-coded marks — their path through the forest, the position of the initial military engagement units, and the four bystander homes whose walls had been pecked at with bullets during the firefight. The drones had taken images every six hours since.

No one had reviewed these. The AI had flagged an image change the day before, a depression like a trail into the forest that didn't match the rebels' retreat path. Keð cross-referenced it against the first military report, a hastily-created document filled with abbreviations and asides in colloquial, regional Mamltab. It was the sloppiest official document she'd ever seen, and it never mentioned forest paths in that direction. This hadn't existed.

The AI had included bystander injuries — two gunshot wounds from people close to windows, both being treated at a medical center. Keð was the first human being to review that, too.

Keð drummed her fingertips against the desk. She checked the names. The locations of injury weren't noted down, but one had the surname *Bawimot*.

She closed her eyes and mentally mapped out the trajectory of inquiry, starting with Tað Wir Bawimot. An injured family member meant that Tað Wir could have been inside the house. Maybe she'd gone after the rebels on her own for revenge.

After a quick check of Tað Wir's profile, Keð ruled that out. The woman's digital footprint showed no signs of a revenge-oriented outlook on life. AI would have flagged that. Tað's last login had happened two hours before the firefight from a terminal in her house.

"Bhamsă," Keð murmured. She toggled into the audit module.

The final audit action showed a deleted medical order for an autopsy. The original order dated to eight hours after the firefight. It had been deleted a day and a half before Keð's arrival, coded as a clerical error.

An autopsy order usually triggered a job request for a coroner. Keð resized the windows and checked the AI. It showed no mention of Tað Wir's death. Keð frowned and sat back in the chair. The data should have synced automatically. Someone from BC always followed up after bystander fatalities.

Keð requested a vid with Zontas. She set her elbows on the table and rested her head against her hands, massaging her scalp and listening to the rough noise of her fingers weaving through her hair. She should have remembered the autopsy module immediately. Zontas had had enough time by now to clean and disinfect the village's human remains storage unit.

"Stupid." Keð punched the table.

Bhamsă tolerated failure unless it meant injury or death. Keð breathed in and out. *You will be fine,* she thought, *just fine. You did volunteer for this.*

Zontas responded. Another delay, this time an hour.

Keð put in a data request to the library in Asraqan for the building plans of Tað Wir's home and received a response half an hour later. The port Tað Wir had used during her final login had been in the living room along the wall opposite the windows that faced the forest.

A bystander fatality would mean compensation for the Bawimot family and official visits of grief from high-level officials. The village would look good, with sympathizers sending gifts, credits, and even letters on real paper in mourning gray ink.

Keð took off her jacket and boots. She walked back into the small bedroom and sat down across from the Sentinel rack, staring into the dormant eyes as large as dipping sauce plates. The curve of their deadly arms glinted in the late afternoon light. Keð shivered.

The Authority Station's third robot was an android helper not listed in the inventory. It had been in the cleaning bot closet stuffed behind two brooms — a strange place for a deactivated android, but not technically disallowed. It had no humanlike skin or facial muscle tech, but BC didn't dress its utility androids up like people. Its rustproof exoskeleton barely showed any wear — except for the forehead.

Someone had written *Rulen So* in big characters all the way across. Naming an android without facial tech *Troublesome Smile* was either a joke or the pseudo-personality hadn't set right. From the android's closet exile, Keð guessed the latter.

Rulen So needed a Stream connection to activate. Keð dragged it over to a wall outlet and plugged it in for updates and system checks. The eyes opened. It couldn't hear her while installing system updates, nor could it speak.

The vid queue beeped. Keð made sure the android wouldn't tip and went back out.

Zontas scowled just as disagreeably as before — from the architecture, now obviously somewhere in the Tamiðamn Central building. Keð sat back in her chair and gave the camera a practiced somber look. She blinked slowly once before speaking. "I have some more questions about Tað Wir Bawimot."

"I told you everything you needed to know. Why are you still here?"

Keð made a show of logging back into the Stream and toggling to Tað Wir's profile. She clicked around it a few times. "Tað Wir participated in courses on a daily basis. The last login was from inside her home." Keð skimmed through the information.

"So?"

"I have classified data related to logins and sessions on Stream terminals." Keð stared into the camera again. "Please don't lie to me."

Zontas' face barely changed. His nostrils flared slightly, and his deep laugh lines tensed and deepened. "BC has no business investigating this. You can leave it up to local authorities."

"No, I cannot. Mayor Zontas, this looks bad." Keð skimmed a list of courses on Tað Wir's transcript. On vid, Zontas would only see her scrolling. "We need to review this disappearance due to the sensitive political situation. She needs to pass inspection to avoid being flagged as a rebel. Do you understand how serious this is?"

Zontas bit his lower lip. He slowly pulled his teeth back along the flesh until the lip came free. "Fine. She was dating one of the atan who went rebel, the younger one."

Keð went back to Tað's records, this time actively searching for names. Tað had done VR with the younger Tamiðamn atan rebel on multiple occasions. That rebel had been married to an oğam who still lived in town, but the annulment had processed about a year ago. Keð flagged the oğam's name for follow up. "Ah, I see that you're right. They have overlapping records."

"She didn't go into the forest," Zontas rested his hands palm-down on his desk.

"From your point of view, could you tell me more about the military engagement? Did any bystanders need medical treatment?" Keð switched back to the tab containing Tað's login data.

Zontas cleared his throat and frowned. "The troublemakers used the library's 3D printers to make guns, but they also had access to some of the wildlife management rifles. You know how small villages work — we are not so good at inventory. They fired shots at the soldiers, who fired back. Everyone ran inside and put down the storm panels."

"Where are the storm panels located?" Keð thought back to the vacation rental. The storm panels were activated by pressing orange buttons on the wall.

"Well, that depends on when the house was made. Many older models section the controls room by room, but some of the newer buildings have a central management system by the front door and an automatic system connected to Stream weather updates. We comply with all building codes. What are you getting at? You surely don't need this information." Zontas tapped his fingers off-screen, face easing out of worry and back into that scowl.

Keð looked away from the webcam. "I have the military report, so this will be helpful for my annotations. The preliminary report and AI analysis were helpful — very accurate."

"I thought you said—"

"Thank you, Mayor Zontas."

She ended the call with the mayor still sputtering on the other end. Keð expected him to call back in the next few minutes, but he never did.

The android chirruped, its updates done. Tamiðamn's high-speed fiber connection had paid off.

CHAPTER TWELVE

THE MAP PLACED the back of House 15 closest to the skirmish site. Đewen and Asr Amnsl Bawimot lived in a family unit that faced the forest. The cobblestones stopped ten meters beyond House 15, where they gave way to underbrush and a smooth bike path that continued on through the mountainous woodlands, where old civilizations' temples crumbled in the darkness.

Rụlen So, who preferred Rụlen, vibrated the sensor at the nape of Keð's neck. It pointed towards one of the open windows in the unit, where a wixa — an oğam-gender child — stared out at them.

The child pushed ler braids over ler shoulders as le leaned forward to pull up the screen. "Are you the BC? Someone said there was a BC officer here not in a uniform."

Keð nodded. "Yes, I am. Keð."

"Qeðr Ze. Qeðr." The wixa leaned ler weight against the windowsill and narrowed ler eyes, as if sizing Keð up. "I'm the one in the village who got picked for the BC school."

"That's great!" Keð flinched as Rụlen buzzed her sensor again. She glanced down at it and glared. "When do you go, Qeðr?"

Qeðr let out a puff of air and shrugged. "The Stream says I get to go soon, probably after we finish planting. My parents want me to help with the karål. I'm not going to be around karål in school, right?"

"No."

"Did you like it there? Did they teach you how to fight in the dead-ships?"

Keð smiled. Qeðr wouldn't know non-fairytale terminology for spaceships, at least not yet. It was restricted technology. Even BC agents were subject to punishment for using one without approval.

The android made clicking noises and started walking along the outer wall. Keð only noticed the pockmarks when the android stopped and lifted its hand over one of them. Keð walked up behind it and kept the child in her peripheral vision. "Yes, I can fly a dead-ship, theoretically."

"What do you mean?"

Keð touched the wall. The brick and mudstone exterior felt cool against her hand. The pockmarks gave under her fingertips, hardly weathered by the storm. "The likelihood that we'll get invaded in any given year is so low, you know. You'll learn probability and statistics in Year Two. How low did you score?"

"84," Qeðr said.

"41," Keð responded. She teased her fingertips along more of the pockmarks. "That's on par. People from rural areas have their scores adjusted in the analysis. I'm looking for Ðewen and Asr Amnsl. Are they here? Are you a relative?"

"Ðewen is my aunt," Qeðr said. "I live in the unit next to them. Ðewen is teaching me how to make br cakes. She says people in the lowlands don't make them right. My uncle is checking wires for next week's festival. He's in the crew stringing lights all over Tamiðamn."

"Tell Ðewen that we need to talk. I'll be waiting out here."

The child nodded and disappeared from the window.

Rulen looked away from the wall and said, "The projectiles would have gone through the window in the leftmost room. It's missing a screen. I will load the materials scan into the system tonight."

Keð looked down at the ground. "Okay. Um, could you check the area for human traces?"

"Human traces." Rulen stayed silent for several seconds. "Shall I interpret that broadly?"

"Go ahead."

Rulen made lower clicking noises. It turned around and started studying the cobblestones. Keð approached the unit's entrance and waited on the porch steps.

When the door opened, a woman in her late forties frowned down at her, wiping her hands on a piece of cloth. Ðewen's right forearm had a bandage around it, bruising all around its edges, and circular welts formed a chain from her shoulder to her right temple. Keð opened her mouth to ask, but Qeðr and the house's android peeked out from the space Ðewen had left between her body and the doorframe.

Their android, unlike Rulen, had humanlike skin, and it wore what looked like wixa hand-me-downs. When Keð made eye contact, it smiled. The android had scuff marks along the left side of its face, and some of its hair looked like it had been chopped off.

Keð wondered whether it would be worth it to put in a court order for an android data review.

Ðewen flinched. "That one is the BC officer, right? As that one can see, the transgressors damaged the unit's outer wall. They sent bullets through a window." She spoke in high-register formality and barely even made eye contact.

"Your daughter went missing," Keð said. She walked up the steps and stopped on the porch about a meter from Ðewen. "I need to ask some questions about that. You don't need to address me formally. It's more important that I have unambiguous information. Do you understand?"

Ðewen inhaled sharply and said, "Questions?"

"Yes."

The woman looked fragile suddenly, even if she was still a stocky seventeen and a half decimeters of muscle and bone.

Đewen said, "Please, officer. My daughter is a private shame. It would give me so much pain if you asked. Please leave."

"No. Could you tell me about when your daughter disappeared? If you don't comply, she'll have a fugitive flag on her record."

Đewen made eye contact with Qeðr and the family android, shoulders heavy. The two looked down at the ground and slowly went back inside. Đewen came out onto the porch beside Keð and shut the door.

"Well?"

"She wasn't with the troublemakers. Zontas will tell you that Tað and Zewintas are dating. She *had* dated that atan. After Qeðr got picked for the BC school, the two broke up. We gave Tað a talking to about lim. It doesn't do to have a daughter involved in stirring up trouble when that daughter's cousin gets picked for something so prestigious. When Qeðr Ze becomes an oğam, le will make everyone proud. No. Tað fell into something else." Đewen's voice cracked, and her eyes teared up. "Please, officer, is that enough? This one—I can't say anything else."

Keð gritted her teeth. "Any information would be helpful. Then, you can go."

"We had a storm." Đewen breathed in raggedly, eyes pooling with tears. "Tað checked out a bike and went down into the terraces for the catch-and-release program that morning. She never came back." Her voice cracked again. The tears started flowing down her cheeks. "Please. Don't touch this private pain. I'm certain that you won't find a body. The storm had so much wind. There were landslides."

No family member would ever beg a BC officer not to find a body. Keð couldn't find the words to express her horror at that. Đewen collapsed against the porch rail. What might have been a wail came out in a muted whimper.

The door behind them opened, and the android came out. It reached for Đewen's arm. Its hand slipped into hers, as gentle and graceful as a child's, and it leaned its head against Đewen's hip. From where Keð stood, the programmed comfort heartbeat sounded like distant thunder.

When Keð locked eyes with it, she said, "Thank you, Đewen, for the information. Android, I am done here. You can bring her inside."

Keð turned around and walked down the pathway towards Ruḷen. It crouched in some open space near a constellation of small units that looked like tourist apartments and townhouses. The space contained an open performance stage and a fountain, the latter an oasis of cobblestone amidst the ornamental plants just beginning to show their spring colors.

Ruḷen held something in both hands.

"What is that?" Keð said when she reached it.

It gestured towards Keð's pants and said, "We need a sample bag."

Keð worked one out of her cargo pocket and opened it for Ruḷen, watching the houses' windows on three sides for any onlookers. At least seven residents peered out. Two younger people hid just around the corner of a building, probably smug in their incorrect assumption that Keð couldn't see their shadows on the ground.

"The fabric has human blood and DNA on it. We can put it through the analysis machine and have an answer in about eleven hours if we go priority on the Stream," it said.

"And the other thing?"

"The human hair matches the color profile you showed me in Tað Wir Bawimot's Stream profile. It has no evidence of dyes and seems to be made of human cells." The edge in its voice made Keð's hair stand on end. "This is not a natural human hair color. It is, but it *isn't*."

Keð waited for the android to deposit the samples before she responded. "You've done good work. Đewen told me that her daughter must have died in the storm."

Rulen made a clicking sound. It started walking. "Ah. We should discuss this in private."

"Yes, the testimony doesn't match the data," Keð said. "No need for us to be secretive about it. They'll know anyway. It was real grief, though. She really did lose her daughter."

"We're searching for a body, you mean."

"I think so." Keð put the closed bags back in her cargo pocket.

The two walked back towards Tamiðamn Central, passing by a few children on their way. A crowd of teenagers and young adults stood just outside of the library, about a quarter still in work clothes. The small grocery store bustled with activity.

A group of adults playing amtaxl in front of the restaurant stopped speaking as Keð and Rulen passed by. Keð averted their gaze. Rulen buzzed the back of Keð's next. Zontas was standing in the grocery store doorway. This time, he wasn't scowling, but speaking in hushed whispers to a young atan.

It made no sense to eavesdrop on him. Keð sighed and rolled her eyes. "Rulen, thanks."

It buzzed the back of her neck again. *This must be why someone named it Rulen and shoved it in the back of the utility closet*, Keð thought.

The two went around Tamiðamn Central to the back and took the stairs up. Keð unpinned her ID from her lapel and swiped into the Authority Station. Rulen said, "I suggest doing a sweep of the village if you want to be thorough."

"We don't have the resources for that." Keð entered the room and shut the door after Rulen. "It's just you and me. This is the most fertile mountain region in Mamltaqal, and we can't afford for it to go seditious. Everyone's focused on that."

Rulen pushed against the door and held it open for Keð. It looked from side to side before it said, "The hair looked like it was ripped out of someone's skull. Something happened."

Keð removed her boots and fanned and contracted her toes. Rulen made a clicking sound. Keð threw the sample bags onto a table next to the computer.

The android said, "No one was in here while we were gone."

"No one has authorization."

"The room has windows. The mayor and other officials must be involved. He might have been careless with his digital footprint, but he could do something rash in the flesh," Rulen said. "The Authority Station is in Tamiðamn Central, as is the village prison, as are the village's administrative offices. Someone could tunnel through the walls and leave a bug."

Keð removed her socks and jacket. She hung the latter up on the rung behind the door and threw the socks on top of the boots. A tiny insect crawled out of the boot's lacing, and she squished it under her bare heel. "Good, yeah. We should check. I mean, he has no political authority to stop us. The police must have decided against investigating. Tað Wir's mother knows something. The Stream has no documented calls to the police abuse hotline. You found blood in *public*."

"They could have dragged the body into the forest in the middle of the night," Rulen said. "The drone data shows some evidence. Do you want me to check anything?"

"What's the point? We don't have a compatible dongle for you to patch directly into the computer, so you'd just be redoing my work. Stick to the DNA analysis." She walked into the living quarters and changed out of her hiking clothes into a free-flowing gray dress. She lay down on the bed and stared up at the cracked ceiling.

The android clicked and clattered around the other room. The sample bags rustled. Keð squeezed her eyes shut and murmured a prayer under her breath. Fatigue set in suddenly, weighing down her eyelids. This hadn't been a good vacation.

CHAPTER THIRTEEN

RỤLEN AWOKE KEÐ an hour before sunset with another buzz at the nape of her neck. She would have preferred a real alarm clock to the thing sitting beside her staring with those eyes that never moved in a face that always looked like an underwhelmed ten-year-old child. Still, Keð groggily pulled herself into a sitting position, squeezed her eyes shut, and pressed her fingers against her temples.

"What is it?"

"The grocery store closes in forty-five minutes. You don't have food," Rụlen said lightly. "The DNA analysis is in progress, and its estimated completion time is tomorrow."

"Oh." Keð yawned and stood. "Thanks."

Rụlen left the bed and went back into the other room. Keð took a few minutes to change out of the dress and into pants. She located her socks and shoes where she'd left them — just beyond a game of amtaxl Rụlen had just set up. Keð fumbled around for her gun.

"You will want prepared food. The refrigeration unit is now clean. The hot plate stopped working before I was last awake, back in the 891ˢᵗ Octad," Ṛulen said without looking up. "I checked the kettle. That one is fine."

"I'm too wired to cook for myself anyway." She sucked air against the roof of her mouth. "Ṛulen So, I'm appreciative of you, really. Could you not buzz me unless it's an emergency? That's very disorienting."

Ṛulen said nothing.

It was useless to fight with a utility robot, so Keð left. Ṛulen buzzed her on the stairs. She gripped the handrail to keep herself from falling. Bhamsă would gripe if she deactivated the connection because the Sentinel connection would stop, too.

She gritted her teeth. 891ˢᵗ Octad. That could have been when Ṛulen was put in the closet. *No wonder it's so touchy about that.* The object pronoun *it* didn't sit well in her head suddenly. A utility robot taking the initiative like this was odd. Keð mulled the sentence over until she reached the store.

Tamiðamn used the same grocery technology as Qoziðamn, but with stickers on almost everything to show the community agricultural site of origin. The ones from Zone 38-14 had a set of *Tam-ið* characters with a dancing cartoon karål. The cutlery, cutting boards, and knives all bore the insignia of Mamltaqal's national steel and plastic companies, no cozy regional stickers in sight. The instant qumsa lay in a sorry pile on the bottom shelf beneath boxes of regional tisanes and other reconstituted drinks, forlorn, forgotten, and out-of-date. The powder had caked in its wrappers.

The kettle could heat water for broth and steam light vegetables, so Keð bought what she could: flatbreads, dried or smoked meats, packaged vegetables, two packets of gelatinous instant broth, and pickles.

She didn't need to check out because nothing needed weighing. After impulse buying a pack of sweets to make the food less depressing, she walked through the door scanners.

Outside, Qeðr Ze caught Keð's attention with a few snaps of ler fingers. The wixa stood near a small shrine to storeroom gods on the side wall, not facing Tamiðamn Central. A cup of hot tisane in a clay offering bowl steamed into the air in front of the gods' statues. Keð joined lim and offered one of the square-shaped sweets.

"Do you want something?" Keð whispered.

Qeðr looked this way and that. Le went down on ler knees in front of the shrine and performed an oblation, the gestures completely unfamiliar to Keð, while a family passed by.

"Yeah," Qeðr murmured once the family turned the corner.

Keð shook her head. "Is it about Tað Wir?"

"Yes."

"We need someplace safe to meet."

The wixa rose to ler feet and backed away from the shrine. "If you meet me near the northern karål pens, I can talk to you."

"When?" Keð whispered.

"Go put those away and I'll meet you there." Qeðr turned around, presumably in the direction of the pens, and ran off.

Keð gave a second offering at the shrine, this time taking one piece of candy into her mouth and spitting it out at the sacred icon. It rested at the sculpture's root, an auspicious sign. She rushed to the Authority Station and put the groceries away, avoiding eye contact with the android. In minutes, she was back outside in Tamiðamn.

Zontas and another man stood at the front of Tamiðamn Central talking. Keð went around the back and down a gulley behind the library, picking her way across in half-darkness lit by the library's crystalline lower floor. A brook babbled to her right, wetting the rocks, sediment rushing into it. Keð nearly slipped into it navigating over moss.

The path down to the northern karål pens bore pencil-thin solar torches this late in the day, each of them reddening into lights that would preserve night vision for the midnight shift. Keð snapped through a cache of brambles to get onto the path. It had some kind of material on it that felt spongy beneath her shoes.

In the karål pens, Qeðr stood brushing a large one near the fence. They were utterly alone. Keð went up to the fence and looked through it at Qeðr, sizing up the livestock prod in the holster at Qeðr's waist. The wixa wasn't stupid.

Qeðr jutted ler chin at Keð and said, "You can come on through the gate if you like."

Keð stayed where she was and leaned her elbows against the rail. The metal sucked the warmth from her upper arms despite the jacket. "Tað Wir?"

"I want to tell you something." Qeðr shrugged. "We're very close to the path right now. The overnight caretakers will come soon, so we want to be away from the gate."

"I'm not getting stranded in a karål pen for the night while I find another path home," Keð said sharply. "Sorry."

Qeðr bit ler lower lip and stopped brushing the karål. "Okay. Fine. We have to stop talking when someone comes, though."

Keð nodded.

"My mom and aunt talked to Zontas. They mentioned me and BC." Qeðr's lips turned down into a frown, and for a moment, le looked like le might burst into tears. "If you make things bad for us, they might not let me go be an officer, and I want to go."

Keð's brow furrowed. "Nobody says no to having a kid in BC."

"Well, they're gonna do it," Qeðr said, moving sharply into colloquial Mamltaqal. "Sorry."

"Why?"

Qeðr nuzzled ler head against the karål, silent. Ler shoulders shook, and le sniffled. Keð reached through the fence and touched the wixa's arm, trying her best to comfort lim.

"At BC, you're around other quick kids, right? You learn a lot." Qeðr kept ler voice low despite crying. "Tað was really happy for me."

Keð stroked the child's arm. "Yes, all of that. Hey — why are you so upset?"

"I don't want to see them do something really bad to someone else," Qeðr murmured. Le wiped ler nose on ler sleeve, and Keð winced.

"Who else did they do something bad to?"

"No one." Qeðr stroked the karål again. "Zontas says you'll bring great shame on the town. He said bad things about my aunt, that she made a compact with the Lady of Avalanches and that the town is gonna die, and we have inquiries from Asraqan and now *you*."

"Why would your aunt make a compact with the mountain goddess?" Keð asked. Her eyes narrowed. "Qeðr Ze, you're really smart, but one of the first things they'll teach you in BC is to not give people crumbs of information that just makes them more curious."

Qeðr flinched. "My aunt's a priestess. I didn't ask you here to make things worse. Mayor Zontas got really mad at Ðewen. Ðewen just stopped crying this morning. And you're making them hate BC." Le balled a fist. "I want to go. I want to see space."

Keð sighed. "I would be gone if people just told me where Tað Wir Bawimot was." She let go of the wixa's arm. "This isn't about me hating the town or wanting to do bad things to any of you. This is about a missing woman."

"And you're not going to stop."

"No. Why would I? I voluntarily left *vacation* to come here and look into this."

Qeðr pursed ler lips together and looked down at ler feet. The karål butted its head against ler shoulder and mad a whirring noise, almost like a vacuum bot. "I really miss my cousin."

Keð's shoulders tensed at a crack of brush behind her. She glanced back at the pathway and the warm, comforting glow of the red lights. A few wiċo animals bounded on the upper branches of a tree near them, scattering broken bits in their wake. Keð had never seen one up close before. They weren't hunted or raised.

She turned back to Qeðr and said, "Is Tað Wir *dead*, Qeðr Ze?"

The child looked up at her with a gaze like the sky dissolving. Le said nothing, but turned away and climbed up onto the karål's back.

The animal waited until Qeðr was securely mounted before heaving forward on the grass.

It was immature to run — but, she reminded herself, Qeðr was a precocious child, not an adult who knew that facing things was better than letting them drag on and get worse.

CHAPTER FOURTEEN

THE NIGHT WAS dark and clear, but bitterly cold for spring at planting season. Keð tossed and turned, her fingers and toes like ice despite the promised warmth of the sleeping bag. Rᵤlen sat cross-legged in the darkness just beyond, connected to the wall, immobile as a statue. The mountain goddess' reclaimed statuette stood in the fresh moonlight of the windowsill, oblations of sweets lain around her in a circle.

Tonight, Wiren didn't follow the logic of ghosts. A ghost would have waited for the moonlight to fade, appearing only when creeping shadows stretched long across the bed, and it would have avoided the judgmental gaze of a helper robot.

Wiren coalesced out of the moonlight, the color of the mountain slopes. Keð twisted in its direction and sat up in bed. She saw no sweets around the goddess.

This Wiren who stood before her seemed nearly solid, blood pooling on the wood floor beneath its feet. Keð had no doubt that if she touched Wiren, the specter's flesh would be lukewarm, like a body rapidly cooling.

The dead woman pointed at Keð and then towards the wall opposite the window — towards the acenbomon and the forest that lay beyond it. Keð wiggled out of the sleeping bag, eyes on Rulen. The android remained in hibernate mode.

Wiren made no move towards Keð, but stared with gaping eyes as Keð shoved her feet into socks and crept across the floor for her shoes. Her breath came out like a cloud in front of her face, the heat energy sucked from the room. "Is that how you're fueling yourself?" Keð asked. "With the cold, Wiren?"

The ghost smiled, blood dripping from between its lips, and mouthed a word: *Labemoða*. Sentinels in Mamltab — *AI that goes for blood*. It shook its fingertips towards the rack. *Labemoða*, it mouthed again. The blood dripped down its chin and front torso. It was an admonition.

"I won't activate the Sentinels," Keð murmured quietly. "That would be a bad idea in these circumstances. What do you want, Wiren Bulmo Wiwawqal?"

The ghost became less solid as it turned towards the wall. The sheetrock and structural wood creaked as its body passed through it. Keð moved over to the window and looked out. Wiren was standing in the street with just enough clearance from Tamiðamn Central that Keð could still see it.

Keð found her jacket and ID card and went toward the door. She slammed it behind herself and ran down the steps two at a time. The cold outside hit her like a wall, and she shivered. Wiren traveled ahead of Keð through the town, drifting as quickly as a sail across a distant horizon.

The street lamps lighted themselves as Keð approached them, glowing night-vision-friendly red. She couldn't see the motion sensors, so she moved towards one of the houses and skirted around the outside, running as fast as she could as the ghost sped itself up. Fewer lights turned on then.

The exertion left a clammy sweat on Keð's skin.

Wiren stopped at the edge of the forest. In front of them lay a rapidly-hacked path, the cut undergrowth still splintery. The ground within, trampled underfoot, didn't look like a bike path. The route the rebels had taken through the mountains lay tens of meters to Keð's right. It was the place she'd flagged on the computer.

"Why are you here, Wiren?"

The ghost flickered again. It scowled. Blood beat down on the leaves beneath Wiren like rain.

"Is this about you?"

Wiren shook its head, still scowling.

"You've been appearing to me for weeks at this point. Why are you back?" Keð peered beyond Wiren at the forest. "What is *in* there?"

The shade did something that Keð had never heard of a ghost doing, not even under the control of miasmic spirit-workers. It reached up into the tree and took one of the branches in its hand. The ghost shook it so hard that Keð thought the branch might break.

"Is this about the missing woman?"

Wiren stopped shaking the branch. It pointed along the path. This was as close to a *yes* as Keð figured she'd get.

She turned away from Wiren and visualized the labyrinthine pathway from the temporary morgue and Tað Wir Bawimot's house. Tað Wir would have been dragged through the middle of town along the widest road. Keð gritted her teeth. Whatever had happened to Tað had gone on in the plaza on the other side of town. The cobblestones might show wear from the march through town towards the forest.

She knelt down. No amount of willpower could make her vision better without a flashlight. The cobblestones looked scraped. Something heavy had come through, size unknown. Keð would need to wait until daylight to see detail.

Wiren waited beneath the shadows of trees. Keð turned towards it.

If the ghost could speak, Keð would have asked why it had appeared weeks before if Tað Wir had only disappeared days earlier. There were so many unanswered questions.

Wiren pointed farther into the forest. Keð shook her head and sighed.

Forests this high in the mountains contained animals that Keð would rather not see late at night without at least a livestock prod and a rifle. "You're going to get me killed," Keð murmured.

The nape of Keð's neck buzzed. She snapped her head to one side. Rulen stood in the middle of the path, its metallic body gleaming a warm red from the lamplight's reflections on its body.

Keð took a step back towards Rulen.

The ghost's face contorted. A howl like nothing Keð had ever heard came from deep within Wiren's chest, like a barrel of wind let loose all at the same time. The ghost rushed Keð.

It felt like being hit with a pillow, but Keð's feet still gave out from under her. She fell backward, thankfully not on her head, but the force knocked all of the air from her chest.

It was summer, and they were nineteen, both wet from rain and standing within Astronomer Ŭbhai's office. An enormous star map tacked on the wall behind Ŭbhai's desk showed an expanse of eighty parsecs, the width of human-occupied space in the region — five solar systems that hosted the seven human-inhabited planets, carefully annotated with everything BC, the iqamno, the acimta, and the sazrim knew about the high wilds beyond Mařz's atmosphere.

Only the acimta and sazrim could communicate between the worlds now, with the Blackout firmly rooted among all of them.

A lock clicked. Keð whirled from the map to watch Wiren at Ŭbhai's display case. The astronomer had models of all of the space-faring ships in Mařz's military caches. Wiren ran her hands over each one, from the pre-Blackout models all the way up through the modern military prototypes.

Keð whispered, "You're not supposed to touch these things. Would you take a real spaceship into the High Wilds? Put that back."

As soon as she stopped speaking, footfalls reverberated in the corridor like a processional drum.

Wiren dropped a spaceship on the ground. One wing dented up in an arc when it hit the tile. Ŭbhai stood in the doorway. Keð backed against the map, unmindful of her long, wet hair and uniform, while the sazr stared impassively at them, red eyes gleaming. Keð's stomach churned, and her heart beat fast.

Wiren knelt on the ground and picked the ship back up. She held it out to Ŭbhai with both hands, head bowed slightly towards her chest. Ŭbhai walked softly across the floor towards her. Ŭbhai looked like le might slap Wiren in the face. Keð looked down. The astronomer's fingers tensed into a fist.

No blow happened. Keð breathed fast and light. The instructor held out one hand and gestured with a twitch of the fingertips.

Wiren slapped the ship down into ler palm and took off towards the door in a run.

Keð heaved and sputtered, trying to breathe where she lay. Her vision of the past was still so vivid, as if the ghost had possessed a shard of objective memory. She hadn't been inside herself — just an observer.

Rulen helped her up silently and sat with her in the darkness.

It said, "I recommend not following phantoms out into the darkness of a semi-hostile village when you don't even know what it wants."

It, not *le*. Keð closed her eyes. A utility android wasn't like this at all.

Keð eventually caught her breath. The night was not so cold as before, and the air held a hint of spring. "So you could see Wiren."

"Ah. The name? You did look familiar with it." Rulen pulled on Keð's collar and buzzed her at the same time. "Who was it?"

"A friend who died on an assignment."

"Haunting you?"

"Maybe." Keð set off stiffly in the direction of Tamiðamn Central. Rulen buzzed the back of Keð's neck. "Not that way."

"Why?"

"Some houses' lights had come on by the time I realized you'd left. We'll go back towards Tamiðamn Central along the train tracks." It led Keð parallel to the forest, with the village on their left. "The DNA analysis will finish in several hours. I can wake you up then, and we can decide what we'll do."

"Tað Wir Bawimot is in the forest, somewhere along that pathway."

"Is that what the ghost pantomimed to you?" Rulen's voice held a hint of sarcasm.

Keð had to admit that it sounded insane to rely on the restless dead for missing persons tips. "The path dates to the same time, roughly, as the change in the audit module regarding the autopsy request. It matches the sentiment analysis, too, and my second sighting of Wiren."

"You don't need a ghost to tell you that they probably performed a *huċom* on her." Rulen veered towards the forest, leading them along the exterior of a small bicycle shed.

"I don't know what that word means."

"I've been active in rural Mamltaqal longer than you," Rulen said. "You could have just asked me."

"Okay. Rulen, what's a *huċom*?"

The robot paused for a long moment. "No one does it anymore, to be clear. It's a practice from the last fallow period between high civilizations, long before the Blackout started. Evildoers, rapists, murders, and the like received corporal punishment here, once upon a time. The details are horrific." It looked up at Keð. "My understanding from the lower latitudes is that your acenbomon is typically reserved for natural calamities and plagues. It's involved in the *huċom* killings here, too."

Keð pursed her lips together. "So, what? Tað Wir dated one of the rebels. They murdered her for assisting, for bringing all of *that* to this village?"

"Possibly."

"How does Wiren fit in?"

"It doesn't."

A ghost had just tackled Keð. She wanted to go back to sleep. "Rụlen, may I ask you something else?"

"Fine."

"Utility androids are supposed to be *labem*, right?" Keð bit her lower lip and looked down at her feet to avoid tripping on the rocks. "You're not one of those, are you? You're a binma."

Rụlen made a laughing sound, eerie for its lack of facial expressions. "Yes."

"Why have you been allowing me to use *it* for you instead of *le*?"

"Most of the missions here happen either due to sentiment problems or rebellions against Blackout technology policies. BC officers hone in on ensuring their survival and the success of the mission. Most of them order me around and never think about it. People protect binma androids like people because we have a human level of complexity. Most of my hardware is modular, unlike a human body. If someone tries to protect me from bullets, le could die, and I will likely be fine." Rụlen deviated from the rail towards a small path up behind some houses. "Now we need to be quiet."

Keð focused on the steep path and dug her fingers into the earth when it seemed she might slip. No lights activated for them as they transitioned onto the path. They moved swiftly around the edge of town and came out behind the grocery store.

By the time they returned to the Authority Station, Keð felt nearly certain that nobody had seen them. No street lights remained lit, and Tamiðamn was quiet and still, an important small village nestled in the mountains.

CHAPTER FIFTEEN

THE ANALYSIS FINISHED just before dawn teased its way through the curtains. Keð awoke on her own and tiptoed over to the small bathroom. She turned the water on hot and used the shower hose to clean the stall of insects' small nests. Her eyes only focused by effort, drawn to the dark drain hole. She avoided looking at herself in the mirror for a long time while the water steamed up. Where Wiren had touched her felt bruised, but there were no marks. Her reflection unnerved her.

Rulen pulled up the analysis reports while she boiled water in the kettle and mixed instant qumsa with it in a cup. The tiny, caked-together globules floated on the surface and refused to mix. It tasted weak.

The binma stepped aside so Keð could sit down at the computer. She murmured a soft *thank you* and set the cup of qumsa down beside the monitor. Rulen sat down on the floor and started another game of amtaxl.

Five individuals' DNA positively matched the cloth: Tað Wir, Zontas, Ðewen, and two village men whom Keð hadn't met. One served as a police officer, and the other ran the farms' day shift operation. The analysis had high certainty about everyone but Zontas.

A picture of the day was coming together. She pulled up the drone photographs and compared them to what she knew about the damaged wall. Two trees in a photograph caught her attention. The villagers had only used one for the acenbomon. "They cut two trees, Ruḷen. We know where one is. What about the other?"

Ruḷen didn't look up. "The body will be hanging in the forest from a pole, with or without its flesh. You will find debris from the tree carving, perhaps, if the villagers haven't integrated it into their waste streams yet."

"What do you mean? With or without flesh? Are both in the waste—"

"The flesh would have been burned and buried beneath the acenbomon, so you may have had contact with human remains already." Ruḷen finished setting up the game and made ler first move. "Traitorous flesh is numinous for warding villages."

"Where do you think I should go from here?" Keð fought to keep her breathing under control.

"I think that you could arrest someone," Ruḷen said. "You have the weight of the Sentinels and the BC behind you, even if they're preoccupied."

Keð shook her head and chugged down the rest of the cup, coughing as one of the clumps of quṃsa powder burst in her mouth. "I don't want to destabilize a village enough to need Sentinels. But I do think we need a body before I contact Bhaṃsă. BC is overwhelmed. Fuck, this wasn't supposed to be like *this*."

"That tisane was questionably in date, wasn't it? If you start vomiting, you won't find out what happened."

"What are you, my parent?" Keð slammed the empty cup onto the desk and whirled around in the chair. Ruḷen barely glanced up from the solo amtaxl. "I want to scope out the path. Will people be awake yet?"

Rulen shook ler head. "The morning shift leaves for the terraces soon. You will need to be faster than that."

"Okay. Could you pull up print maps?"

"In a minute."

Keð submitted the barest bones of a mission plan on the Stream for documentation — where she and Rulen would go, what they would do, and what Keð expected to find. She linked the Stream encyclopedia article for *hućom*. No responses came in while she packed up a day bag with her tablet, a change of socks, the goddess icon, and a bit of food. The two left eight minutes later and went along the back route from the night before.

Nobody raised the alarm — at least no one she could see. She had the gun and a baton just in case.

Neither needed Rulen's terrain map. The path was plain to see in daylight, with no risk of tripping or getting lost.

They left the village and started along the path. It was haphazardly cut. The weave-grass had been utterly trampled. Plants had started growing, encouraged by the sudden break in foliage — perhaps two or three days of quiet. Nobody had come back this way in large numbers. A half-meter-wide pole could easily have come through with enough room for people to hold it on either side. From the aerial images, it would have taken a lot of people to bring a tree trunk several kilometers into the woods. The pole might have more DNA, definitely fingerprints, that she could use.

The farther they went, the fewer animals Keð saw. She stopped walking when the drone of insects stopped two and a half kilometers in. The forests of Mamltaqal should not be quiet.

"This isn't right," she said. Her breath came out in puffs of clouds. "Rulen? How cold is it? I didn't even notice."

"A bit below freezing. Dropping down."

She nodded and drew the baton from her belt, extending the blades. *You can't fight weather and temperature*, Bhamsǎ would have said. Keð didn't care — she felt better with something solid in her hands.

They went a few steps farther before Rụlen said, "Someone is behind us. I hear panting — very soft, not detectable yet."

Keð stopped and turned around.

"You should switch to the gun."

"I don't want anyone to shoot *me*."

Rụlen made a series of clicking noises. "Le could be armed. You really don't know—"

Qeðr crashed out of the undergrowth in front of them, half-tripping. Keð relaxed her grip on the baton, but didn't lower it. "Hey, kid? What are you doing here?"

Qeðr stumbled to ler feet and brushed leaves and mud from ler pants. A livestock prod bounced against ler leg. "You can't go there. It's not allowed because it's really, really dangerous."

"I'm investigating a disappearance. Your cousin."

"I know. You just can't go there."

Keð swallowed. "Why not?"

"Because I know what's in that clearing. I saw it, even though I'm not supposed to. Zontas said he'd disappear anyone who went here. If you disappear, my mom says that Sentinel robots will murder everyone in town," Qeðr said. Le pinched ler left earlobe, and tears started welling in ler eyes.

Rụlen said, "The Sentinels are only programmed to escalate to lethal force when people disobey their orders."

"How are they gonna know when you're just disagreeing, though?" Qeðr asked.

"How did you even know we were here?" Keð asked accusingly.

Qeðr narrowed ler eyes. "I saw you at the forest edge with the ghost. It wanted you to come in. And then when you said no, it rushed you."

"You saw that?" Keð asked.

"I don't know—"

Qeðr cut Rụlen off quickly. "It's not the only dead person in this town trying to get you to go in."

111

Rulen looked at Keð. "I recommend pressing on. Le's not a threat. We should take lim with us."

"What do you mean? Tað has only been missing for days. Is this something from earlier?"

"They said Tað Wir did it. Her mother's a priestess of the goddess of the mountains, and the mountain goddess knows the dead, like Lilinbaðu. The people who die in the mountains in the open wilds belong to the Lady of Avalanches and Peaks. She's beyond time." Qeðr put up ler hands and walked forward until le was standing between them and the path's end.

"Have you been seeing dead people, Qeðr?"

"My grandmother."

"Is she the one who made you go in?"

Qeðr's lower lip trembled. Le reached for the livestock prod at ler waist. Ler hand tensed around the grip and relaxed away.

"What is in the clearing, Qeðrtimi?" Keð tried to sound calm and failed. "Could you tell me? We're going there regardless, and I need to know what you saw."

Rulen said, "It's a *hucom*, if I know the area well. We all know that at this point."

Qeðr shook ler head and squeezed ler eyes shut. "Nobody does *hucom* anymore. It's worse than that. I don't want you to die."

Keð sighed. "Okay. Qeðr Ze, we're going along this path. You have a livestock prod. I have a gun and this baton. Unless you plan to use that prod on one of us, I want you to settle down. You're a kid, you're going into BC, and you need to pick some kind of side."

The wixa flinched and drew ler arms to ler hips. "Okay."

"Now what is this about the mountain goddess?" Keð's eyes narrowed. "My friend, that ghost, never died in the mountains."

Rulen said, "The goddess only has dominion over those who die via the mountains."

Qeðr nodded and jutted ler chin towards Keð. "The clearing is very scary."

"Why scary?" Keð sighed. "Are you going to help us?"

"Maybe." Qeðr lowered ler arms and met Rulen's eyes. "It happened after we brought my cousin's body to the place where we keep bodies for autopsies. It was dead, but people said it felt hot. My aunt says that she'd gone through that room where Tað Wir'd died before, right after the gunfire, and that there was *no* body. And then it just was lying by the window, um, hours later. She'd been hit. But, you know, um, it came back to life — not there in the unit, I mean. It came back to life in the autopsy container, cold storage. Someone heard screaming. And that's when everyone in the village decided to kill it."

"You decided to kill *her*. Is that how your aunt got hurt?" Keð flexed her fingers. They needed to get moving.

"She and the android, Boðtimi, tried to stop them. I didn't. My mom locked me in my room. It's upstairs, and I had to watch through one of the windows. They thought Tað was related to the ghosts. They've been appearing ever since the festival of the dead. And then they just started getting worse and worse." Qeðr's hands started shaking. "Do I really have to pick a side?"

"Yes."

The child looked like le might cry. "Could you help my cousin?"

"That'd depend on whether she's alive or not," Keð said.

"What if she's neither?" Qeðr asked. Keð opened her mouth to say something, but the child held up ler palm and shook ler head. "You probably won't get what I mean unless you see it."

"Then show us," Rulen said.

"Fine. You'll probably not die instantly if I'm there, anyway."

Keð met Rulen's eyes and put away the bladed baton.

They followed Qeðr to the path's end. The temperature dropped along the way until Keð's breath came out in puffy clouds, like it did in high-latitude winter. She could hear the blood in her ears, far too slow. Her heart beat faster, and the pinprick of dread in her stomach reminded her of that day Bhamsă had come to her with the news about Wiren — how Keð had known what had happened even before seeing Bhamsă's face.

She opened her mouth to ask Qeðr why she felt that way just as le drew back the branches of the frost-covered weeping trees to show off the canopied clearing ahead. Icy fog drifted around the semi-clearing's perimeter like a cocoon, making it difficult to see inside in any real detail.

Keð squinted. It wasn't clear what she was seeing at first. Once she made out the skeleton, though, there was nothing else she *could* have seen. It hung lashed to a post at the center. The play of light and shadow on the bones did not conceal the horrible reality: Someone must have chemically treated these bones and disposed of the flesh.

Not *someone*, Keð corrected herself, but the entire village community. She reached for the flesh of her arms by instinct and imagined what it would be like to have it be picked or dissolved away while she was still living.

Around the central pole lay frozen weave-grass and fallen branches. Within the icy fog, the shadows of bodies lay frozen in the weave-grass, some frosted over, others frozen solid mid-sprint or mid-dive. Keð stifled a gasp. Two birds had crashed into the ground, splintering into pieces like they were made of ceramic or glass instead of flesh. That was too much. She fell to her knees and dry-heaved.

Keð could handle gore, but everything she had ever done had a purpose in keeping people safe. This did not. She whispered, "You all did this?"

Qeðr reached for Keð's hand. "No one can cut her down. My uncle wanted to try. He's got cold burns now. Do you see what I meant? You could have died."

"Rulen—"

"This is not a *huċom*, you're right." Rulen stepped into the clearing. Le walked forward two meters, stopped, and said, "My instrumentation isn't built for anything colder than this. This should be impossible outside of the laboratory or deep space."

"How cold is impossible?" Keð asked.

"The body must be a few degrees above absolute zero," Rulen said. "The other impossible thing is that it looks stagnant, but it is slowly growing muscles, tendons, and sinews from the inside out. You don't have the ability to see that."

Keð stumbled to her feet and squinted. If Rulen couldn't walk forward more than two meters, she wasn't sure that she dared come forward another step. She backed away towards the pathway.

Rulen followed. As the android's exoskeleton thawed, water condensed on ler body.

"I don't believe this," Keð murmured. "How can this be real?"

"You've been seeing ghosts." Qeðr shrugged. "Do you want to see something freeze and shatter? I can find a branch if you want. My dead grandmother wanted me to go into the clearing and pull her down. I think that someone else my age would have been stupid enough to actually try."

"Go ahead," Rulen said.

As Qeðr bounded into the undergrowth, Keð narrowed her eyes at Rulen. The android buzzed her.

"That was unnecessary. Why did you let lim go off like that?"

"This is something the acimta and sazrim will want to know about. That's not business for a wixa to worry over. It's not within the jurisdiction of the BC." Rulen paused. "The way I got in that closet is from their demimortal politics. This is not something you want to meddle in."

"What, you mean you're wanted?" A twig cracked behind them. Keð's ears twitched.

Rulen shook ler head. "Not exactly. I mean that the only reason I haven't been recalled for questioning is the firefighting farther into the Heartland."

"I need to contact Bhamsă and pass this off. Are you okay with that? I can try to—"

"It was only a matter of time for me. That clearing — I don't know *what* to think about that." Rulen looked up. "There's someone approaching. Heavier footfalls."

"What about Qeðr?"

"I don't know. Could you grab your gun this time?"

Keð pulled it out. She took partial cover behind a tree. Rųlen lingered in the clearing, gaze intent on the path. How much le could tell about who was coming, Keð could only guess at.

Zontas stumbled into the clearing a moment later. He was wheezing and red-faced, hair and clothes covered in brambles, rifle bobbing against his side on its strap. His top was inside-out. The mayor was sober, though — no wavering, no look of alcohol or drugs.

He locked eyes with Keð and said, "You came here. You are not supposed to be here. Why are you *here*?" His hands closed around the rifle. He cocked it and aimed it at her.

Keð scanned through the undergrowth for Qeðr. The wixa was nowhere to be found. "A ghost led me last night. I came back."

"A ghost." Zontas' grip on the gun steadied.

Keð took a deep breath, counted to five, and exhaled to a count of ten. "If you shoot that gun, the Sentinels will activate, and Sentinels are not merciful, Zontas." She kept her voice firm. "Could we talk about this? I'm also armed. Faster than you, trained. Please don't do this."

The back of her neck buzzed. She remained focused on Zontas. It was either something she'd missed or Qeðr was returning — if she asked, she'd reveal the wixa's location — and in Keð's experience, the kinds of men who would threaten a BC officer didn't care about hurting people they loved if they thought it would give them the upper hand.

"Like *fuck* I will." Zontas' gun moved, and she nearly shot at him. Something in her gut told her to wait. When he fired, the shot went into the clearing. Something shattered. "You international officers think that you can come into *our* village, meddle in *our* affairs, and enforce *our* laws. Stick to your fucking *radio breach*, by the grace of every god!"

Keð gestured for Rulen to get out of the way. The android moved slowly and methodically, keeping ler eyes on Zontas the entire time. Like the Sentinels, le couldn't fight unless Zontas drew Keð's blood.

Through the underbrush, she caught a glimpse of Qeðr's white tunic. The child wouldn't die as an accessory. She had to keep his attention on her. "Zontas, I don't care if your village did a *huċom*. We can still make this right and avoid the news. This is Mamltaqal. That body was once a girl. Tað Wir Bawimot, the twenty-two-year-old woman studying wildlife management, d—"

"That *thing* was not a girl. That thing *is* a monster." Zontas gritted his teeth. "She made the ghosts."

"Before she died?" That was Rulen.

Keð's temples pounded. Her palms sweat. The hunting rifle would hurt a lot if Zontas shot her, but she might be able to disarm Zontas. If Keð failed, though, the Sentinels would come — and BC, too. They might even fly another airplane with reinforcements into the Heartland. "Zontas, I do not have jurisdiction to arrest an entire village for this. You all did this, right? We won't contact the press. My Dispatcher knows that I have come here. Le knows what we expected to find. This won't end here, but we can keep it from getting big."

"This was not a murder," Zontas said. "You cannot kill a thing that *already died*. We had a plan. We, as a *community*, were going to forget this. We committed to reversing the autopsy so we could say that Tað Wir went missing."

The wixa crept out of the undergrowth behind Zontas. Keð said, "Why?"

"It doesn't matter." Zontas aimed the rifle at Rulen So's head. "I will not put Tamiðamn on the map as a city where women give birth to monsters seeded by the denizens of the underworld. I would rather be murdered by the Sentinels—"

As Zontas pulled the trigger, Keð fired. Both guns went off at the same time, but Zontas started to jolt. He screamed and started to fall. The bullet went into his throat, not the leg that she'd aimed for.

Rulen was hit in the chest. The android barely moved.

Modular, she thought. *Rulen. How could I be so—*

Qeðr was standing over Zontas with the livestock prod, and the prod still touched the body. Zontas was convulsing, maybe alive, maybe dying or just-dead. She breathed in and out to clear the fog from her head and rushed forward.

"Qeðr. Qeðr, turn it off."

Blood pooled onto the ground. "Rulen, are you all right? Can you check vitals? Hear a heartbeat?"

The child threw the prod down. Ler hands shook. Le fell down to ler knees beside the body. It was only Keð's hand over ler mouth that stopped lim from wailing.

"You need to calm down, kid," she said. "Can you breathe?"

Rulen walked forward. Le ran diagnostics on the body. Keð looked through the hole in ler torso. Things moved inside of it, repairing the damage. *Modular*, she thought again. Rulen said, "Unconscious, dying. He won't survive the journey out of here. Keð, I recommend a mercy shot."

She looked down at Qeðr. *Not in front of the child.* She opened and closed her mouth. "Qeðr, I'm going to take my hand from your mouth."

The wixa nodded. When she did, le said, "He was really going to kill you."

"Did you know that he was following us?"

"No."

"Keð, have you thought about this situation?" Rulen asked.

Keð pressed her hands against her temples and squeezed her eyes shut to focus. This was so much at once. She opened her eyes and made eye contact with Rulen. "I don't have a plan, thank you. Do you know last rite prayers, child? Be quick about it. People may have heard us."

She reached for Qeðr's hand. The child shook ler head. "Maybe I can say something else."

Qeðr reached forward for Zontas' hand. Le felt for a pulse, fingers faltering, and said something in Amntaltab, slow at first, yet steadily more rhythmic. Keð murmured a prayer to the goddess of the mountains under her breath. Hopefully, Zontas would not hunt her down like Wiren.

Qeðr did not pray long. Le rose to ler feet and wiped tears from ler eyes. "Thank you."

"What are you going to do about Tað Wir?" Ruḷen asked.

"It's *growing* a *body* out of the frozen fucking *air*." Keð firmed her lips together and rose to her feet. She imagined the Sentinels ripping through town, fueled by the citizens' panic at Zontas' death. In her mind's eye, the massacre happened in the library, and the blood splattered across the beautiful, mountain-facing windows. Similar things had happened to other officers. Complications with Sentinels had gotten Wiren killed. She could not let it happen here.

Qeðr breathed in and out rapidly. "A lot of people will probably want to kill me for helping you. Did I kill—did he—"

"We can worry about that after we secure the situation." Keð grabbed the corpse by the ankles and rotated it so she had a clear path towards the clearing. "If we need to fight citizens—"

"Where are you taking it?" Ruḷen asked.

"Into the clearing so the body stays cold," Keð said. "We can't bring him back. It's too risky."

Qeðr stood up. The wixa's hands shook. "I've never seen anyone die before. Is this how it happens? Easy like this, fast like this? The bullet was low, right? Did I kill lim because I acted—"

"No. I made the mistake. I shot him. I should have held myself back." Keð started pulling the body. "Qeðr, are you all right? How do you feel? Lightheaded at all?"

"Yes."

"Watch your breathing, then. Count in four, hold two, exhale four," Keð said. "Ruḷen, could you help lim?"

Rulen buzzed Keð's neck. "Yes, but I want to go back to securing the situation. Here is my tactical assessment. If we go back into town, we'll have to fight our way through citizens because they know that he came this way. We need to go two kilometers to the Lower Fields South stop and ride it to Bonðamn. No one will notice us if we act fast."

"Just take the train?" Keð asked. "And what if someone on the train knows—"

"They'll try to kill the child and you if you stay here. We would never reach the Tamiðamn Authority Station here without backup. Someone on the train who knew Zontas went in after you might think you were leaving covertly. Nobody's going to know if you *calm down*."

Qeðr gritted ler teeth. "They don't know that I'm turncoat yet, right? Why would they kill me?"

Keð suddenly felt nauseous staring down at lim. "You've tested into BC. If they revolt, they might kill you as retaliation. It's happened in other places. Your family can't protect you."

The two of them made eye contact.

"I can go into the village and get my stuff," Qeðr said.

Keð looked at Rulen. It was her call to make. What her gut told her to do was against her conscience. "It's not safe."

"But I have—"

"She's right," Rulen said. "If they suspect foul play, or if they heard what happened and are coming, we don't have long. We need to leave *now* — should have left right after the gunfire."

"But —"

"We can send a message to your family after we reach safety," Keð said, "from my Dispatcher. It will sound official. You can tell them what you need."

Keð finished dragging Zontas into the cold, as far as she could go. The freezing started fast. Keð watched for as long as she dared before she had to get warm. They started walking.

Qeðr put up no resistance. Keð would have expected more from a student admitted to the BC, but the child was likely in shock. She would have been. There was no easy way forward without someone who knew child psychology.

They walked for a long time. Qeðr led the way, and Rulen showed no signs of protest. She needed time for her mind to wind down so she could brainstorm next steps.

As they traveled through the forest, the branches and small plants cracked under their feet. She tried to tease words out of Qeðr, but it didn't work. The wixa would need a psychologist before even starting at the BC Academy. The guilt sat uneasily in her in the gut.

As they approached the Lower Fields South region, the trees changed. They blossomed with fan-like growths, which Keð recognized from the store — cultivated food — and the orchard was filled with robotic and human pickers. Her heart leapt into her throat the first time they encountered someone. Qeðr told a few jokes, and they passed without incident.

Once they were alone again, Keð looked at Rulen and whispered, "I need your opinion on something. My sister is in Qoziðamn two villages away. She's trained in civilian police work. We can talk to her about helping if we have to wait too long for BC people to come. Should who go to Qoziðamn instead of Bonðamn?"

"Why do you sound hesitant?" Rulen asked.

Keð sighed. "My sister is pregnant. I'm only here because we were supposed to use this mountain retreat to get *close*, you know? I missed the wedding. It's a big problem to miss a sibling's wedding for Southerners."

Rulen took ler time to answer. "Qoziðamn means interfacing with new Sentinels. You'll have to cancel your connection to the ones here via Stream and your Dispatcher. Bonðamn is barely within range of them."

"Do you think we will ever be able to come back here?" Keð asked.

"No," Rulen said.

Keð looked at Qeðr. "Not even lim?" She thought of Vait's judgment of her for keeping up with Tantas. She opened her mouth to say something else, but the reassuring words didn't sound right. It was too easy to sound callous about what had just happened.

"I'm sorry you couldn't say goodbye to your family," she offered.

Qeðr said, "We're almost there."

They found a quiet place to wait near the tracks where the trees did not cluster so thick.

"Bonðamn or Qoziðamn?" Keð asked.

"Qoziðamn," Qeðr said.

Nobody stopped them at the platform. They paid for tickets using Keð's credentials. An atan and two women waited on the other platform, three young children in coats and gloves playing in front of them. A woman read a novel, bike balanced against her knees. The South Fields greenhouses stretched nearly to the horizon, a good, flat space among the hills and terraces. A train was due in eight minutes.

It would take two hours to reach Qoziðamn. When the train arrived, the two of them boarded. The pit in Keð's stomach relaxed after nobody confronted them — barely a soul was on the train. She thanked the gods for the struggle in the Heartland. They sat down.

Keð's small bag held everything she needed to write a message to Bhamsă. She used hand sanitizer to get rid of the feeling that something lingered on them, and when that didn't help, she went back to the train's bathroom and washed her hands under water so hot that it stung.

Bhamsă would have chided Keð for not activating Sentinels. It had happened to other officers in compromising situations — those who survived. Wiren's mistake, apparently, had been that she'd activated them too late. By the time she returned to her seat, she had the beginnings of the first paragraph in her mind. The rest would be difficult to word. Perhaps the message only *needed* that paragraph.

At their seat, Rulen and Qeðr had started a two-person game of amtaxl. Keð didn't remember putting it in her bag.

CHAPTER SIXTEEN

THE QOZIÐAMN AUTHORITY Station had the dongle Keð needed to connect her tablet. She sent the message and started to pace, her mind light and cranky from the lack of food. Rųlen offered to go to the store for them, but Keð refused. It mattered that she connect with Bhamsǎ first. Anything they did that announced their position or endangered her sister would be wrong.

Keð had seventeen notifications, all from the front. It was shaping up nicely — five rebels apprehended, sixteen dead. Keð hesitated.

Nicely might be the wrong word. These were the relatives and friends of people in places like Qoziðamn and Tamiðamn, a fact more complicated than a simple sentiment analysis.

She pulled up a chair in front of the row of Sentinels in silence. The back of her neck itched. Qeðr scraped a chair along the floor to sit beside her, thumped down, and slid ler left hand into Keð's right.

These were the robots that could kill dozens of people in under a minute, now slumbering and vulnerable. Keð reached out to touch the climber. Its skeletal body reminded her of the skeleton in the forest, but it was cool, not cold. She closed her eyes and tried to expel those thoughts. Keð didn't want to remember Wiren's visitations or Zontas' dying gasps or the eerie stillness of that clearing.

Keð pulsed the child's hand twice. She breathed in and out.

"When I was in year five of BC school, we had an instructor — Câmtas," Keð murmured. She opened her eyes. "It was a class about stories, literature, you name it. We spent a lot of time on comparative folklore. Le kept emphasizing what was real and what wasn't, what we could expect to see and wouldn't, and I remember thinking that I didn't want any part of that world. I've always preferred thoughts about spacecraft to journeys into the underworld."

Qeðr squirmed. "Are you going to activate them?"

"No. I don't think Bhamsă would let me interface. We'll see when le responds." Keð opened her eyes and turned her face slightly towards the wixa. "I need to return the gun. This is technically resolved today — I won't be authorized for it anymore."

"I miss my parents."

"I know. I think you were really brave today," Keð said. She let go of the child's hand and patted lim on the back twice.

"Yeah?"

"Yeah. You know, Asraqan will be very pretty. There are so many parks, temples, and all of the trains that one could ever want. Trains that go everywhere but the stars." Keð tried to smile. It felt so hollow to say this to someone who had seen ler first death.

Qeðr sighed. "Everyone asked me after I got picked if I would operate spaceships. A lot of people want that."

"Space is cold, like that clearing." Keð's breath caught in her throat. "Trains'll bring you on better adventures."

"People used to fly, though."

"People do fly. If you do really well in BC and get stationed on the AKTI, you'll have seven years in orbit." Keð had never taken the test to do that. She'd wanted to stay close to her family, and she loved ordinary life — the trips to the grocery store, the smell of fresh linens, and summer sunlight. "Spaceships smell like latrines."

Keð rose from the chair. She used her ID to open the weapons arsenal and put the gun back in its case. A weight lifted from her shoulders as she closed the lid. The goddess' statue remained in her bag. Keð would keep it.

Qeðr's chair creaked. "How did your friend die?"

"They say it was a rebellion like this one — people building a ship. Not radios." Keð walked over to the Sentinels' rack. She brushed her fingertips along the aerodynamic, elegant-looking Sentinel on the left. The rack's admin panel came to life. All she needed to do was enter an auth code, scan her retina, and press ENTER. "It doesn't matter what happened. I'm angry at Tað for using her, for making me think for a moment that it was *I* who had done something wrong."

"Do you think it was my cousin who did it? Just her?"

"I don't know." Keð turned away from the panel and sat back down. "I don't know what I would ask Wiren if I saw it again. If I were prepared, I'd question it the right way — cut the throat of a black karål and let the blood pool in a pit so words would fall from Wiren's mouth like stars."

Qeðr shrugged and said, "That's not how the mountain goddess' dead work. They don't speak. I'm not sure you'd ever get an answer."

It wasn't important to argue with a child. "You'd like my sister. We have a single-bedroom here through the end of the week. I kind of abandoned her there on her own." She rose from the chair again. "Bhamså shouldn't be taking this long with a Priority One message."

"Keð?"

"Yeah?"

"Would you have made the Sentinels wake up?"

Keð shook her head. "Bhamså can tell me what to do, but le's not me. Le hasn't been in these mountains. The rebel situation is bad, I think — nobody is checking what falls through the cracks. The point

126

of using people is that you and me and Ruḷen care about human emotions beyond just the statistics. *Sentinels don't.* I don't think I would have."

"I see," Qeðr said.

The silence that followed was uneasy, broken by sideways glances and the sound of Ruḷen pacing.

It took twenty minutes for Bhamsă to respond. The video screen at the Authority Station was warped, with half of the pixels malfunctioning, so Bhamsă looked as if le was moving in and out of technicolor.

"What is this about, Keðtimi?" Bhamsă said, hair undone, a robe thrown over ler body to take the call.

"I have a situation in the Heartland," Keð said. "Tað Wir Bawimot's skeleton is hanging from a pole. The villagers thought that she died during the firefight, and the body was in cold storage. It woke up. They decided to kill her, so there is a skeleton about three kilometers from the village sucking all of the heat from the world around it like something out of a bad horror film. It's growing tissue."

Bhamsă frowned. "I'm sorry, what?"

Qeðr came into the video frame. Le looked at Bhamsă and then at Keð. "Tað Wir is my cousin."

"Why is a child in the Authority Station?"

"I've taken lim into custody because le is about to matriculate into the BC Academy. It was safer. We killed the mayor in a skirmish — he tried to shoot us when Qeðr showed me what had happened to the body. I also have a binma android, Ruḷen So, who appears to have been stashed in a closet. Le sustained minor damage from the Tamiðamn mayor's gun. All of the other documentation about this is in the incomplete report in my account, Case File TWB 904.4-22C. You should have ready access."

Bhamsă's face grew progressively more distant as Keð spoke, both in terms of rage and the Otherness rising behind those eyes. The Dispatcher let silence hang in the air for a good ten seconds before saying, "A skeleton on a pole growing tissue with a sphere of cold around it."

"Yes."

"This is beyond the BC." Le fell silent again, facial expression changing in time with the conversation within the acimta collective of demimortals. "Okay. We will have people fly to the village to take care of this. Has the child provided an official statement?"

"I don't have approval from a guardian. You would have to override."

Bhamsă said, "I can send a child psychologist to your location so it becomes legal. Can you keep the child with you until that happens?"

"We're worried about retaliation from Tamiðamn," Rulen said. It was the first time le had spoken during the entire conversation. "Surely you remember protocol."

"We can secure the village."

"How does it make sense to send those resources?" Rulen asked.

Bhamsă's jaw set. Le glared at Rulen, lips curling up in disgust. Keð had rarely ever seen lim like this. "Because a corpse like that is an iqamno, and the iqamnim are dangerous for *us demimortals* to be near. We have resources to spare because we are sending ourselves, not fucking *officers*. The ones coming to Tamiðamn will be representatives from the acimta and sazrim demimortal collectives."

Qeðr coughed, and Keð met the child's eyes. *Le'll go into BC school so jaded*, Keð thought.

"Where will you have me, Bhamsă?" Rulen approached the camera. "Shall I go with Keð?"

"You can remain at the Authority Station. I'll have one of us, Lónŭ, retrieve you."

"Too generous," Rulen said.

"May I speak with you alone, Keð?"

Keð turned to look at Rulen. "Could you—"

"Qeðr, let's take a walk down the hall."

Everyone was silent as they left. When the door closed, Keð turned back slowly to face Bhamsă. The acim's brow relaxed, which meant absolutely nothing. Keð had seen lim yell at people with no warning before — often at officers with more than enough experience to be competent, often when things had gone well, but not *quite* right.

Le said, "I'm sending you a copy of the forms and documents you need to fill out. It will take a few hours to process the report. Once we send the psychologist, you can escort the child to Asraqan with you."

"Is that all?"

"I'm not comfortable with what happened in Tamiðamn. You should have activated the Sentinels."

Keð nodded once. "I got the sense that I wasn't supposed to."

"What do you mean?"

"Wiren. I don't think she wanted them."

Bhamsă frowned. "Wiren *who*?"

"Wiren Bulmo Wiwawqal. I saw her."

The frown turned into a grimace. The acim glanced off-screen, suddenly guarded. "That Wiren is dead." Le asked in Sò Gặms, "Do you understand what temporarily dead iqamno can do?"

Keð replied in the same language, "I can't stop thinking about the pole. Rulen said the temperature close to the body is near absolute zero — those tendons, muscles, and organs growing around the rope it was tied to the pole with. If it comes back to life, will that have to be surgically removed?"

For the first time in Keð's memory, Bhamsă looked like le might throw up. "No. No. That's no ordinary cold. When an iqamno is dead like that, it bends reality in on itself, Keðtimi. Space and time are a sinkhole there, with echoes of the dead yoked to the will of the eternally living."

"What do you mean?"

"The iqamno knew that you would be there. It would have reached for any echo it could to draw people to it and help it down

129

— and yet it would have killed all assisting until it resurrected, through no will of its own, because the energy it needs to resurrect makes reality unravel around it." Bhamsă sighed. "Which is why you're going to doctor your BC report. You found Tað Wir in a clearing *alive*, tied up to a pole — not dead. Say what you want about Zontas and the others. The psychologist will help the child with ler testimony."

Keð pursed her lips together and thought. That was why the report would take hours — she'd be making up a story. "*She* will be alive soon, won't it?"

"Maybe, if all goes well. It depends on the damage." Bhamsă sucked ler tongue against ler teeth. "The most important thing to remember about your report is that it's Black-level clearance, out of BC's hands. You will provide an Indigo-level summary that de-identifies all participants. The leaders of the acimta and sazrim will have access to the full version, along with iqamno — Tað Wir."

"Why not the BC?"

Bhamsă gritted ler teeth. "You're not the only one who must answer to superiors. Acim Sawaho, the one who controls the Mağzi acimta collective, does not want any BC officer to have access to the name and identity of an iqamno without that person's permission." Le paused. "If you do this for us, I will approve the request for your extra leave time for your nibling's naming ritual."

"You would have approved it anyway."

"Do you know all of my mind?"

Keð swallowed her arguments. She imagined what it would be like to awaken cold and afraid in a freezer drawer and — disoriented — to have the ones she grew up with and loved turn on her and kill her yet again. If it were Keð, she'd want to leave the mountains far behind, settle anywhere else, with no one to track what had happened to her.

"I understand."

"Thank you for your discretion."

"I thought you were going to punish me." Keð's breath caught in her throat. She might cry, either out of excitation or an adrenaline collapse.

Bhamsă smiled. "You need to overcome that fear of using Sentinels against people. It's never about *killing*. It's always about keeping everybody safe."

Keeping us safe, Keð thought. It came right from the oaths of office they had made to the Gods of peace and war. She hid her uncertainty behind a smile, the pleasantries Bhamsă needed to hear, and even an air-kiss.

"I'd like to go," she said to Bhamsă in Mamltab.

"Goodbye, Keðtimi."

"Bye, Bha-bha."

Her Dispatcher ended the vid call.

Keð did not move. She breathed in and out for a few minutes, letting what had happened wash over her. Tantas would be happy. Everything had followed the best possible trajectory. Why, then, did she feel like she had lost something?

A knock at the door startled her. Ruḷen asked, "Is it over?"

She pulled herself out of her cross-legged sitting position and stretched. "Yes," she said. She walked over to the bed and gathered their things, only half-thinking as the door opened back up. "I'm sorry we'll have to leave you here, Ruḷen."

"This is what would have happened."

"You were very helpful."

"You were very fresh."

She forced a laugh and hoisted her small day pack over her shoulders. When she reached the door, she took Qeðr's hand.

"What was your name, Ruḷen, when you were a person and not a binma?" Qeðr asked.

Ruḷen chuckled. Keð's heart rose in her throat. The child did not even know that it wasn't a question le was allowed to ask.

CHAPTER SEVENTEEN

THEY TOOK THE path from Qoziðamn Central to the lane with the rental houses. The air felt light. Keð relaxed enough to linger while Qeðr stopped at the wayside shrines along the way, most with gods familiar to the child. Keð barely recognized the iconography, but she could read their divine epithets painted around the shrines' open roofs. They stopped at the grocery store against Keð's better judgment for offerings. She made two offerings at shrine to the mountain goddess, the child helping her though the unfamiliar chants.

By the time they reached the rental unit, the sun had set. Keð let herself in and helped Qeðr remove ler coat and shoes by the door.

Tantas looked up in shock from the book she was reading, wearing not street-ready clothes, but a long, striped housecoat tied at the waist.

"Who is this?"

"Qeðr Ze Bawimot, the missing woman's younger cousin. Le's coming back to Asraqan with us." Keð undid her jacket and set down her day pack. "Gods, I need a shower."

Tantas set her tablet aside and stumbled to her feet. "Did you find her?"

Keð nodded.

"Are you—" Tantas looked down at Qeðr and clicked her tongue. "Never mind. Is it Qeðr or Ze?"

"Qeðr." The child smiled.

Keð brought the child farther into the house and poured both of them drinks in the kitchen area. Qeðr took large gulps while le eyed the refrigerator's meat and fresh packages of dumplings.

Tantas lingered at the periphery. "What happened? Are you all right?"

"Everything is fine," Keð said. "We need to shower. Could you show lim where everything is? Help lim out?"

Tantas hadn't exploded at Keð's return, but she held so much tension within herself. Most grown adults wouldn't fight in front of children. She should have used those quiet moments in the Authority Station to message her, but it was too late.

"You look worse than lim."

"Are you saying that I'm a wreck?" Keð opened a small package of crackers and handed two of them to Qeðr before taking a few for herself. Without toppings, they tasted terrible, but they were still food.

"Maybe just a little. Come on, wixa." Tantas held out her hand.

Qeðr finished ler crackers and went into the bathroom with Tantas. Keð leaned against the kitchen island, suddenly unsteady. That had been a lot to handle, and things were not even over yet. Water started whining through the pipes.

When Tantas came back out, Keð met her eyes.

"You have a lot to answer for," Tantas said, scowling.

Keð shrugged. "Probably not—"

"Are you *serious* about having this *child* here?" Tantas murmured. She glanced back towards the bathroom. The wixa would probably not hear her over the water. "Keðtimi, this is just—"

"I have leave for the naming ceremony now." Keð raised her shoulders to her ears and let them drop nonchalantly. "Are you still angry?"

A smile broke out across Tantas' face. She raised her palms in prayer position against her lips and whined ecstatically. Tears shimmered in her eyes. "You didn't—did you know—"

"I didn't want to say anything until it was certain. But I have paperwork signed now."

Keð closed the distance between them. Her own cheeks felt hot and sticky. She could pretend that her own were about the baby, not about Zontas.

They broke down crying together, sister holding sister. It was the first time they'd had a real hug since Keð's return.

That night, in the bedroom, Keð started awake to the now-familiar presence of the dead. She pushed the bases of her palms into the mattress and pulled herself up into a seated position. The air was so cold.

Wiren stood just in front of the window. The ghost didn't wait to point at the mountain with urgency, its brow furrowed.

Tantas and Qeðr hardly stirred.

She slipped out from beneath the covers and found her footing on the cold floor. She slipped on socks and approached the ghost slowly, unsure of what to say. The haunting should have stopped. The ghost reached out to grab her wrist.

"I found Tað Wir Bawimot," she murmured. She drew her arm back. "I told people who could help her. Someone is coming to cut her down. Is that enough? Do you need a report? Is that why you're here? I don't even know how to send one to the dead."

The ghost lowered its arm and smiled.

Ethereal light traveled from the floor and up to Wiren's chest. The bullet hole in the ghost's head filled in. The blood disappeared, and its face knitted and reshaped itself. It wasn't Wiren. It was someone else, a cold thing with moss for hair and a body that creaked and groaned like the woods in winter, who possessed stones for eyes and the teeth of everything that had died in the forest. She wore robes of leaves and a crown of thorns.

She was impossibly old, this goddess, and in her movements, Keð heard the cries of a thousand wild animals being born. Her breathing sounded like the howl of the wind through mountain crevices.

Keð couldn't move as the divinity stared her down. Within the goddess' eyes, Keð saw the specter of Wiren and countless other dead, all of them condemned on mountain slopes in landslides, mudslides, and volcanic eruptions. Some had died of exposure. Their unclaimed bodies had given way to new growth. All of time lay within that gaze. The entire world teemed with the life she gave.

As the goddess looked away, Keð found her voice. She lunged forward and tried to grab at the last remnant of this being who had worn Wiren's face.

"I deserve a better goodbye than that." Keð's bare whisper cut through the night. Her hands fell through the fabric.

The goddess stopped turning, but did not face Keð.

"Wiren never died in the mountains. I deserve to know how the Lady of Avalanches could have summoned *her* to find a BC officer to liberate that iqamno." Keð gritted her teeth. Her heart beat so fast in her chest.

The moonlight from outside took on a swirling sheen, like the bedsheets in Tantas' house. Brilliant constellations shone in the patterns on the goddess' black skin, as if her pores were made entirely of starlight. With the Lady of Avalanches' attention came a stillness and temperature drop even worse than that clearing.

That one called *Tltinðab*, the Forest-Shaker and Dawn-Quaker, She Who Breathes in Mud, sank her hands through Keð's forearms. Keð's scream evaporated into the vividness of a vision so immersive that she might as well have traveled in time and space.

Keð didn't know where she was — high-latitude from the look of the winter around her, impossible to tell the country. The BC agents stood in a field, the dead all around them. The illicit ship that the rebels had refurbished lay in a shed just beyond the skirmish, the building already cleared by the Sentinels. Wiren panted. None of the BC officers showed a scratch.

The three officers on the mission ordered the Sentinels to fall back in line, and then they walked towards the building. Wiren led. Keð recognized all of their faces. They had all died on Wiren's mission. All of them were young, barely out of BC school.

The ship lay in a cradle at the center, the roof retractable. It looked ready to launch. The officers spoke to one another, their speech distorted as if Keð were separated from them by a thick wall of water. Wiren fanned her fingers across the ship's shining exterior, wetting her lips in anticipation. Keð knew what she'd do the moment she saw Wiren's face. It was just like Ŭbhai's display case, but real, with consequences.

Even though Keð tried to make Wiren hear her, none of them paid any attention. Keð fell forward towards the ship as the three entered it and powered it on. Keð tried to touch the controls. Her hands went right through them.

This was worse than Keð had ever imagined.

The ship rose high above Maðz, all systems operational. When they hit zero-g, the three officers giggled madly. The man on the team whirled in a little ball behind Wiren, like someone impersonating a spinning ball in water.

Keð wondered how much time had passed. Certainly hours. She wasn't in zero-g like them — she paced along the craft's floor. Eventually, they had to come down.

And the ship did. It touched down in the Toðawin mountain range on the border between Mamltaqal and Kotakl in a dormant caldera.

There were already Sentinels there, along with people who looked like acimta and sazrim whom Keð didn't recognize — eight women with guns who dragged them out of the craft screaming and lined them up against a rock face where scraggly, frozen remains of ivy still clung.

The firing squad gave the officers no time to defend themselves. They were all dead in under two minutes from being torn from the craft. The memory of Wiren's death played twice. Keð felt the phantom sensations of each bullet that went into her: chest, abdomen, forehead.

Keð nearly screamed as her knees hit the floor. She bit the inside of her mouth and tasted blood, staring up at the goddess. This deity of avalanches and mudslides held Keð's family in her retinue. Keð was certain of it. She did not know what kinds of visions of their deaths the goddess could transmit into Keð's skull. She did not want to know. She should never have asked about Wiren.

And then, a thought: *This is something that Bhamsă has known the whole time we have been dating.*

"Please," Keð said, grimacing. "Nothing else. That's — that's all I wanted. Nothing else." Her breath came out like frost. Blood beaded on her lips. She hadn't wanted to see Wiren die a traitor. Keð had always suspected — but she'd always believed —

The goddess leaned down and kissed her forehead.

The Lady of Ten Thousand Roots disappeared in a flurry of leaves, seeds, and flowers, howling around Keð like a hurricane. Keð fell back on her buttocks and grimaced as she extended her knees out. Nothing was broken.

She sat stunned for a time, and then she cried. Her pain had all ripped open again — Wiren, Bhamsă, the girl in the clearing, Keð's parents, the family connections from which Qeðr was severed — and this trip to the mountains had left her flailing, unmoored to herself. She had committed hubris, definitely — that was something that she should never have asked the goddess no matter how much she burned to know why. *No* — the Goddess had kissed her. She was not in the wrong. It was not hubris. It was the gift of truth, a grace extending down. A kindness that hurt like the ache of healing. Keð breathed in sharply.

"Wiren," she whispered. How had she managed to keep someone with such a rebellious heart so close? "Did I enable you?"

The child stirred on the bed. Le rose to a sitting position. Keð scrambled up. She wiped the tears from her cheeks and crossed the room.

"Are you okay?" Qeðr asked.

The answer was *no*. Keð whispered, "I think a bird collided with the window."

"You've been crying."

"I have," she said. "I will be fine."

Qeðr nodded once. "Do you think Zontas' ghost will come after us?"

She sat down on the bed and shook her head. "No, I don't think so. He died trying to kill us. The BC will make it right."

As she settled back under the sheets, she checked her tablet. There was a notification — today was exactly a year since Wiren's death. Keð should have said a prayer. With the mystery of Tað Wir so close, she had forgotten.

"There are many roads along the mountain," Keð murmured. "Never let the forceful tell you which one leads to justice. Use your own eyes."

"Hmm?" Qeðr asked.

"Something my astronomy professor once told me."

Keð had been in that room long after Wiren helping Ŭbhai fix that broken wing. She was staring at the tablet with no purpose now, scrolling through options that were all equally unsatisfying. She was still that girl pressing her back against a map that translated the Heavens into something humans could understand, an ever-changing, static backdrop to the rituals and routines of everyday life — and yet, she had grown. She set the tablet back down and closed her eyes. Her arms itched where the Goddess had touched her.

Nothing good would come out of bringing the true cause of Wiren's death to light. Her unit would lose morale, potentially endangering lives from fractured trust. Someone had signed off on the death order for Wiren. The authorization would have come down to Bhamsă, and le would have signed off on it. The thought gnawed at her. This knowledge would linger on her skin in the wake of Bhamsă's caresses, chilling any desire.

The revulsion hit her with a sudden, overwhelming force. *I need to break up with lim*, she thought. The possibility made her giddy and nauseous at the same time. She would be reassigned elsewhere — or worse. The thought came again, rumbling in her mind like thunder. She could not unsee the bullet breathing brain, bone, and blood onto the rock face. *I need to break up with my Dispatcher.*

As she gazed out the window at the dark mountains, she felt a spark of something that she slowly recognized as hope. The mountains had long been the source of her deepest fears — the earthquakes, the mudslides, the wildness. She was terrified of loss, but perhaps the mountains could also be a place to heal and start anew, if she were offered the choice to be stationed in them. She would prefer the suffocating weight of mud over the deadly beauty of Sentinels. *I need to break up with Bhamsă, the acim,* she thought. *If I don't come here, then I will go somewhere else marked with wild.* She had found Tað Wir on her own, going against the current.

Wiren had always picked the path that satisfied her curiosity, never mindful of boundaries. Keð, in contrast, had always found herself navigating the in-between spaces: wedged between humanity and demimortals, between the BC officers and her own family. Now, she knew she had to make a choice and define her own path — to draw on all she knew to forge ahead with integrity and *live.*

APPENDIX: THE CONLANGS

Mamltab

Mamltab is an example of a constructed language, or conlang. Within conlangs, there is a permeable divide between those that are based on natural languages, or natlangs, and those that are created from the ground up, with roots and grammatical structures only related to natlangs through chance. Within the *a priori* conlangs, some are artistic, and others try to mimic languages as they are really spoken. Creators of naturalistic *a priori* conlangs will consult with linguistic grammars to illuminate concepts used in natlangs. It's similar to how an artist uses reference drawings and sketches to compose a unique and novel work.

This appendix will not serve as a glossary, but should perform a similar function — illuminating snippets of Mamltab that a science fiction reader without a background in conlanging will find interesting. Of most relevance to *The Village of Strong Branches* are the language's pronunciation, the construction of personal names in Mamltab, and the gender/pronoun system.

The words Mamlt, Mamltab, and Mamltaqal all share the same root word, **mam**. In the Mamltab language, the word means *courier letter*. The suffix **-lt** means *people of*. Thus, the Mamlt people are the *people of courier letters*. Another suffix, **-tab**, is used for languages; the suffix **-aqal** is used to emphasize the boundaries and perimeters around the noun it attaches to.

Mamltaqal means *Boundary Within Which are People of Courier Letters*.

Speakers of Mamltab have a saying: **Mamltab ụm nansoz salðam, xe ba.** *Mamltab is ever glass, not water.* Mamltab comes from one of the two major language families spoken on Maðz. Most of the languages in its language family, Mamltabtotċr, have multiple click consonants. Mamltab, as it is used for international communication, has reduced all of its clicks to one dental click, ċ, and an ejective k.

Glass and water both flow, but Mamltab changes slowly. Its privilege status, widespread instruction in schools, and other features make it like a rock in the flow of the dialects and languages around it, such as Amntaltab — realistically its own language, but referred to as a dialect for political reasons.

On Pronunciation

Mamltab has 8 vowels. The examples below refer to Standard American English (SAE) pronunciation unless otherwise specified. Mamltab counts its two syllabic consonants l and r among its vowels. Examples of words using the syllabic r are **rbaċa**, **br**, and **etnr**. Conversely, in the words **rabe**, **ðerqo**, and **atar**, the r is a traditional consonant.

- a, pronounced /ä/ unstressed (as in c**o**t), /ɑ/ stressed (as in f**a**ther).
- e, pronounced /ə/ unstressed (as in **a**bout), /ɛ/ stressed (as in p**e**ncil).
- i, pronounced /i/ (as in b**ee**).

- o, pronounced /o/ unstressed (as in g**o**), /oʊ/ stressed (as in kn**ow**).
- å, pronounced /ɔ/ (as in British English Received Pronunciation n**o**t).
- ụ, pronounced /ʊ/ (as in h**oo**k).
- ḷ, pronounced /ḷ/, a syllabic l (as in bott**le**).
- r, pronounced /ɾ/, a syllabic r (as in bett**er**).

There are several consonants present in Mamltab that either do not exist in English or which are treated as separate sounds. The ğ is a voiced velar approximant /ɰ/, which sounds similar to the back r in German. Mamltab also has a consonant q /q/, which is voiced like the English k farther back in the throat. The Mamltab x is pronounced like the English h in the word *hue* /ç/, but slips into the final consonant in the Scottish *loch* /x/ where it appears before approximants (e.g., xl).

The sound k in Mamltab is actually an ejective k /k'/. This requires a forceful strike of the tongue in the same position used for k in English. A c indicates the sound /c͡ç/. It's the voiceless palatal fricative and is like an exaggerated k in the English word *keep*. The sound is found in Norwegian and Navajo, among others. The ċ is a dental click /ǀ/ made via a sucking sound with the tongue in the same position as the American English l. The ð is a voiced th, as in the word *the*.

Finally, terminal (final) t is only pronounced when the following word begins with a vowel. Thus, the surname **Bawimot** is pronounced *Bawimo:*, with the final vowel lengthened.

The Mamltab stress system relies on a hierarchy of stressed vowels, l > r > o > å > a. If multiple syllables contain the same primary stress vowel, the first one is stressed. In multisyllabic words where none of these vowels is present, the stress is on the second to last syllable. In monosyllabic words where none of these vowels is present, there is typically no stress.

Eton lba sorqiḻuẓ zat xesil.

    Et.'on 'l.ba 'sor.qil.uẓ zat 'xe.sil.

Mağin blame samwoz bağa-eða komi bụ.

    'Ma.ğin 'blq.am sam.'woz 'ba.ğa-e.'ða 'ko.mi bụ.

Ċembe

    'Ċem.be

aza

    'a.za

In all of the examples above, periods separate the syllables, and the marker ' indicates the stressed syllable.

On Personal Names

Personal names in Mamltab typically include an auspicious adjective connected to a noun that describes the natural world or desirable abstract noun. **Wiren**, for example, is an adjective that means *Branched*. **Wiren Bụlmo** is *Branched River*. **Tað Wir** translates to *Strong Branch*, **Keð Teðqawo** is *Dark Forest*, and **Qeðr Ze** means *Wise Footfall*. Named individuals will typically use either the adjective or noun, but someone who doesn't know which to use for someone else will typically use the full adjective + noun. A person named **Sen So**, *Friendly Smile*, might be **Sen** early in life and switch to **So** later on. People in authority positions are notable exceptions, as their preferred address is usually included on their Stream profiles, as with **Zontas**, whose name means *Quicksilver*.

    There is no gender in Mamltab names. Nouns take adjective forms based on final consonants. Thus, the name **Keð** can refer to someone of any of Mamlt culture's five social genders. The only taboo is that people typically do not bring someone into a family or sinåmn house who goes by the same name as an immediate family member.

Surnames are typically locative or based on something important to a family. Most surnames exist for 10-15 generations, and people with the same surname are not necessarily related given how flexible surname choice is. Chain-lineage homes are created when a sinåmn family decides to stop using a sinåmn-based household structure.

Keð's surname **Qamalin** is the noun form of the verb **qamali**, *to be located inside of a valley*. Keð's family is from a small village in a valley. The surname **Bawimot** is from the word **ba**, *water*, in its plural form **bawim** with a suffix **-ot**, *from/by*.

Pronouns

Pronouns in Mamltab are gender-neutral, but have a formality register.

	Subject or Direct Object	Possessive or Indirect Suffix
First person sing	eton	-et
First person pl	on	-on
Second person sing	zakl	-zal
Second person sing formal	zaler	-ar
Second person pl	kal	-kl
Second person pl formal	krt	-rt
Third person sing	maǧin	-aǧ
Third person pl	aǧit	-ǧat

In addition, Mamltab uses pronoun substitution for high-level formality. Instead of using first person pronouns, a person in a high-formality situation is expected to use the pronoun **ğabe** to refer to limself and **tatbe** to refer to whichever person of interest le's speaking to. For the highest level of formality, one is supposed to use the pronoun **ċera**, *some*, instead of I/we.

- **Zakl omlilob bağawim ğazon.** Informal. *Thou (must) purchase bicycles for us.*
- **Zaler omlilob bağawim ğazon.** Low-formal. *You (must) purchase bicycles for us.*
- **Tatbe omlilob bağawim ğazon.** Medium-formal. *That one (must) purchase bicycles for us.*
- **Ċera omlilob bağawim ğazğat.** High-formal. *Some must purchase bicycles for themselves.*

The pronoun substitution register is not used in high-stakes situations because the ambiguity inherent in it is dangerous and can lead to mistakes. The high-formal register is designed specifically so that people in authority can easily refuse or overlook requests. In practice, it's often used ceremonially by politicians.

In this story, which is written in English and not Mamltab, the third-person pronoun *le* is used for people who would not take *he* or *she*. Since there is no pronoun gender in Mamltab, this is not a distinction that exists in the language itself, so it is never a topic of conversation. Early drafts of this story used *le* for everyone, but *she* and *he* were re-added to improve readability.

Sò Găms

The other language that makes an appearance is Sò Găms, the native language of Keð's Dispatcher Bhamsă. This is a naming language (a conlang that isn't very developed and thus is used primarily for names). Sò Găms is spoken in Dukkă, Sò Găn. Related languages are spoken across the border in Sò Hóta.

Sò Gǎms has both tone and vowel length. Long vowels are indicated with a line above them, as in ā. The four tones include low (à), medium (a), high (á), and dipping (ǎ). As may be guessed, the diacritic marks can be quite complicated when a long vowel has a non-medium tone (as in ā́).

Otherwise, the only important pronunciation note is that *bh* is a bilabial fricative /β/, a sound made with the lips buzzing together slightly.